# Eye Spy

a collection of short stories and poems

Eye Spy

A Bournemouth Writing Prize anthology

First published 2021 by Fresher Publishing

Fresher Publishing
Bournemouth University
Weymouth House
Fern Barrow
Poole
Dorset BH12 5BB

www.fresherpublishing.co.uk

email escattergood@bournemouth.ac.uk

Cover designed by: Nilanjana Bhattacharya

# Contents

# Acknowledgements

Special thanks to Bournemouth University and Fresher Publishing who have made this anthology possible. As well as, everyone who submitted to the Bournemouth Writing Prize, without your amazing stories and poems, this collection would have had no substance at all.

We would also like the opportunity to say thank you to Emma Scattergood who was a shining light in the darkness.

# Foreword

Welcome to Eye Spy, a collection of poems and stories selected from submissions to The Bournemouth Writing Prize 2021.

We, the editors of this anthology, are MA Creative Writing and Publishing students at Bournemouth University (home of Fresher Publishing), who are drawn to the darker side of fiction! Mel is the poet, whose work often explores aspects of grief; Belinda likes to write horror and Nila writes thrillers - so there is a piece of all of us in this book.

The journey through the dark of Eye Spy starts with poetry and 'Brave', written by Georgia Cowley. One of Mel's favourites, it explores depression in an open, simple and honest way. Other out-of-the-ordinary poems to look out for are 'Frozen Feathers' by Joseph Snowden and the striking 'Poetry, n.' by CT Mills, which was awarded The Bournemouth Writing Prize for Poetry 2021.

The short story section offers thriller, drama and crime, as well as horror, mystery and the supernatural. It opens with 'An Maighdeann-Roin' - a timeless tale with an intriguing twist, written by James Skivington. For another classical scary story, turn to 'La Llorona' by Jess Allen, which was inspired by the Mexican myth about a wailing woman whose misdeeds in life have left her spirit trapped on Earth. And 'The Second House' by NGF Clark is a must-read for fans of witches and fairy tales.

If you are looking for something closer to home, Belinda recommends you turn to 'Lost' by Jen Hall, a beautifully crafted narrative that leads you into the life of a very unfortunate woman, and 'Control' by Richard Hooton which immerses you in the aftermath of an abusive relationship.

Crime-lover Nila suggests 'The Red Shoes' by John Ward, a noir-type detective story with a thrilling twist, and 'Cold Dawn' by Molly Lloyd, a story that makes you think twice about getting drunk on a night out.

These, of course, are just our favourites, and there are plenty more gems to discover inside these covers. We hope that you enjoy reading them as much as we enjoyed uniting them here.


Belinda, Nila and Mel (Editors)

# Poetry

# Brave

*By Georgia Cowley*

Once there was a little girl,
Who'd never whinge or pine.
She always had a smile for you,
Her name was Caroline.

When all the other little girls,
Blubbed and brayed and bawled,
They said, "Why can't you be like her?"
Then turn away, appalled.

And when she fell and scraped her knee
They'd rush on her with praise:
"Our Caroline would never cry."
"Our Caroline's so brave."

Until one day small, wirey threads
Of sadness, hurt and doubt,
Sprouted deep in Caroline,
And found no pathway out.

They tangled up inside of her,
They'd twist her, pinch and pull.
They grew and grew all over her,
Till Caroline was full.

Soon the tangled spider's web,
Formed a knotty noose,
And Caroline began to fear,
She'd never pry them loose.

Still our girl did not cry out,
Even as she died,
Keeping in the messy thoughts
We've all been taught to hide.

"How terrible" They all bemoaned
Standing at her grave.
"If only she had asked our help."
"If she only she'd been brave."

# Frozen Feathers

*By Joseph Snowden*

Geese flock down on waters still,
the last before first winter.
Their feathers dipped in mirrored glaze,
with ripples of dark water.

Some can flee and go wayward south,
others too weak, must stay.
The old and injured in autumn's wake,
hold pouches, ready to pay.

Frost trapped feathers choke the throat,
when water turns to ice.
Three-pronged knives squirm then thrash,
then mirrors turn sharp white.

Silent songs in geese who cry,
where echoes cannot pass.
Snow once soft, now hard as ice,
no pick nor beak shall slash.

The geese that stayed now sink below,
with necks that have been wrung.
Nature and her noose for bird's,
stalled records full of song.

\*\*\*

Ice now melted, in summer heat,
reveals an empty sight.

For the drowned birds that sunk,
are gone! Perhaps in endless flight?

# There was never any poetry, just blood

*By Elizabeth M Castillo*

There was no poetry that day; just blood.
My memory now-
a haze, a jumble of that day,
some far-removed anecdote I heard.
from a girl I met on the plane
one day, ( I think she had my eyes),
but she was smaller than me. Better skin,
and still believed all these things,
all this mess,
amounted to some sort of poetry.

There was no one home that day,
just me, and what remained of her.
And perhaps... no. The children? I'm not sure.
There was the staircase, with no banister.
Terrible architectural flaw. Two legs,
visible, from the calves down,
and the crying- always the crying.
That morbid, melancholic sound.
"What now?" went the thoughts, "What's happened
today?"
I cleared the corner, eyes riveted
on the top of the stairs, where she stood wailing,
waving frantically, wrists bared. I'm not sure
I understood. I'm not sure
I knew how to care.

There's no memory of what happened,
just the noise, and the blood.
And the guilt, as I looked in her eyes-my eyes,
as we sat in 31C and D. I should really
have felt something. So much blood, her blood,
the very stuff that makes us. But I've found,
there's only so much a young mind can take in
at any one time. I should
have felt something, done something. Been something.
Been enough. Even now, as I try to stitch the memory
back together, I am convinced:
there was never any poetry. There was only ever blood.

# Custom Crescendo

*By Whitney Glover*

I actually like it
when my bones turn to mush,
when my cartilage curdles,
and marrow turns soft.

I actually like it
when my skin pulls tight,
muscles quiver like violin strings,
taut strands of my hair a bow.

I think I want to love it,
when my heart jumps out of
my throat,
open wide,
and my stomach constricts.

I think you forgot
what happened last time,
I think I remember it for the both of us.

I actually like it
when your voice leaves your body, then
it hits mine.

I actually don't mind it
when your feet take you flying,
and you leave,
for the hundredth time.

# A Peculiar Dream

*By Stewart Arnold*

Such a peculiar dream
it lingered yet raced by somehow
Sitting with old schoolfriends
their names elude me now

But why was I chased
by the man with an angry face?
I tried my very best to run
my feet rooted in one place

I remember falling
from a cliff edge, down an endless dark shaft
with such a thud I landed
Who was it who laughed?

Could it have been the clown
or the beggar at my knees
as we floated 'cross a river
on a raft of purple trees

Three fierce dogs faced me
as I knelt weeping in the rain
Someone said 'there, there'
and tied me with a chain

In a flash, the dream was a shadow
Precious relief was mine to keep,
shaking, 'twas then I realised
I had not been asleep

# The Other Woman

*By Elizabeth M Castillo*

The sun has set, and at this hour,
shadows hang between the daylight and the trees.
There, the sudden scent of blood,
scent of *man*,
carries to me on the breeze, the wind
howling through, falls silent at my feet:
"Good hunting, milady,"
it whispers, then retreats. There is
a darkness in this forest, an end
that rivals death itself,
in the mist about my ankles. Even lizards
know they would do well to hide
inside their hovels, and underground.

Dirt crunches beneath.
Treacherous soil!
Leaves plunge downwards,
to be eaten by the earth.
The naked trees testify, this forest is deadly,
and will swallow you whole. I hear
footsteps racing, running, in thundering lockstep.
Flash of black. Flash of teeth.
There are dangerous games afoot!
Surely it's time to turn back.
Surely it's time to go home.
I am well beyond my borders now.

She can't catch me, she can't catch me,
here, where I lurk and linger on the periphery,

just out of sight, just beyond her mind's eye.
She knows I am here, her veins
course with rage, and vengeance.
But she does not know where.
She is death. She is danger.
But the line has been crossed,
the threat prowls within her marked territory.
She may think I have lost,
but this no longer bears any resemblance to a fair
fight. No, now two legs, not enough.
I drop down onto four,
draw strength from the thousand invisible
heartbeats, the lifeblood,
the microbiome of the forest floor.

There is fear, and some fury,
encrusted under each hungry claw. The hunts
smells of my father, champion long before I
had ever heard of this sport, and I wonder:
would he be proud?
There is sweat at my temples, and my wrists are bound
to stop them from trembling.
I step, crabways, low and feral, without shadow
or sound. Your ears twitch and you shudder,
neck craning to see what you
and I must learn the hard way;
the deadliest thing in here is me.

# Insomnia

*By Yvette Appleby*

2 am / don't worry they said
Daily updates / confusing mandates / pervade / invade
my thoughts
Crash around / rebound / vibrate in my head
A ceaseless form of hell / I even yell SHUT UP to
myself
but I don't listen

4 am / the clock on the bridge chimes / a minute later
the church bell
Never together / they measure time / cement my
sleepless status
60 seconds to the minute / 60 minutes to the hour / 60
hours is two and a half days
Count the ways / 1,680 hours lost
Sleep may dissolve / absolve you from dreams that
might count the cost of endless night
Can I lie / sigh / turn / return to where I started

6 am / day seeps through the window
Cue the spotlight / the glow / birds enter centre stage /
put on a show
Tweeting / no hidden agenda / just calling out the dawn /
I yawn / rub my eyes
Do they sleep / relish the silence in the air / because we
are not there
I ache / shall I stir / move / pretend to be awake / to feel
alright
Sit upright / unwind / be kind to myself / NO

Pull the duvet over my eyes / too early to rise / nowhere
to go
8am one leg out / both legs out
Lift yourself / groan / moan / walk like a Neanderthal to
the kitchen
Put the toast in / look at the phone / message someone
Stay safe is the new goodbye
Answer a message / you OK ?
Me?
Fine, I reply

# "poetry, n."

## *By C T Mills*

/ ˈpoʊ ɪ tri /
1 *literary work in verse*

2 *solace*
in line breaks, i curl
up- in you, i take comfort in the whip and way
of rhyme and

3 *inspiration*
i am denise riley's lover. that is to say, i know her
intimately, which here means too well
we grieve the same, in rags, scrabbling in the dirt for a
glimpse of your soul
were you ever even here?

4 *grief*
is hungry and i feed him sad songs because
my hands are shaking
too hard to cook a real dinner, because night has fallen,
and you are still
not home

5 *i-*

# Undelivered.

*By Nichola Rivers*

Look.
The rain is cutting holes in the sky.
Cold air met warm air
Was bowled over.
Droplets curled gently around dust and smoke,
Became heavy with it.
Little water-parachutes splat above me,
They knock loudly.
I'll let them in.
I see the future; triumphant rainbows.
You had too much sun in your eyes
You chose to close them.
Sleep now then.
The sky sheds its bitterness and so do I.
It pools and flows
Out into the world flows my cold river.
Making new connections.
Concealing the grit.

# Jag Älskar Dig, Auntie

*By Hanna Järvbäck*

This suitcase of mine
Is far too heavy.
It overflows
With the things she left me.
And not a single thing did I want to miss.

Scattered on the bottom you will find,
Jewellery she kept close and always mixed.
Silvers and golds.
If that is not bravery,
Then I don't know what is.

Jammed in the corner are her glasses,
To help me see.
Because one day she told me,
That despite my eyes are green,
I watch and judge with blue,
And that would make it harder to start anew.

In the middle I have wrapped
The things she told me to care for, gently.
Like the left eye teardrops from her sister,
And the blood from the heartbreak of her mother.
The disorientated mind of her husband,
And the very memory of her soul.

And the suitcase is overloaded,
With all the words,
They all had to say.

Of all the advice she always gave.
To never ropa "hej" förrän du är över ån,
And always kolla till bordet,
När du sparkat med tån.

In this suitcase of mine,
I have put in her shoes,
Although in them I will never walk.
And I cried when I packed her last words,
Jag älskar dig,
And goodbye.

# Short Stories

# An Maighdeann-Roin

*By James Skivington*

It was the odour that first alerted him. Of course, they had
often smelled something similar in the few weeks since
they had moved into Rockport Lodge on the Northeast
coast of County Antrim. The salt on the sea breeze, the tang
of seaweed and the driftwood cast onto the beach, odours
that seemed to bring an added vibrancy into their new life,
almost a promise of adventure. Yet there was something
else about this odour, something vaguely familiar, though
he could not think what it might be.

His wife had insisted that they get a house beside the
sea, that she felt so much better within sight and smell of
it. But as the man sat there in the semi-darkness of the big
living-room, his wife away on a visit and his ten-year-old
daughter asleep upstairs, he sniffed the air again and knew
that this time it was different. There was a sweetness there
and a kind of muskiness too that made him wonder if a fox
had passed close to the house, though he knew that all the
windows and doors should be closed against the cold of the
night. And still that nagging feeling that he had encountered
this odour somewhere before. Slowly he looked around
the room and out through the windows but saw nothing
untoward.

They had fallen into the habit of leaving the curtains
open at night so that they could admire the view, the beach
and the sea, not fifty yards away, the dark bulk of the
headlands, the lights of the village across the bay. At the far
window, their Christmas tree lights twinkled up at the stars,
which blinked in reply.  Now and then the moon, emerging
from behind a cloud, threw a pale-yellow beam across the

dark, placid water. The plashing of the waves on sand was so gentle that he could barely hear it.

And then, seemingly of its own accord, a door slowly opened, wider and wider, until it almost touched the wall. He sat forward in his chair, eyes wide, heart suddenly pounding. He strained his eyes to look into the darkened kitchen. Nothing. He looked around him, at the windows, at the fireplace, behind him at another door and, seeing nothing out of its appointed place, began to feel a little foolish. Yet when he turned back to look at the open door to the kitchen, there she was. He tried to stifle a sudden gasp, but it escaped him and seemed to reverberate through the silence. At first, he thought it was his daughter, come down from her bedroom to get a glass of water, for the girl was about the same age, but his daughter's hair had never been in ringlets to the shoulders, *she* had never worn a string of shells around her neck nor a long white dress above black buttoned boots. And oh, that face, with its skin so white and those large, almost liquid eyes. The voice, when it came, was strangely low, almost husky.

"Do you know, sir, where my mother is?"

The man was incapable of replying and simply stared at the girl. She walked slowly across the room and looked down at his daughter's presents beneath the Christmas tree, stooped and ran her fingers over one of them. She let out a low sound, almost a growl, then turned to him.

"Has she come for me, sir?"

"I - I don't know your mother," he managed to say, though his throat was tightening as he spoke. "What's your name?"

"Ursilla," she told him.

This was as a hammer blow to his chest, for that was his daughter's name, insisted upon by her mother. As the man clutched the arms of his chair and was enveloped in a fog of fear and incomprehension, the girl walked across the room and into the kitchen. After a moment's hesitation, the man leapt from his chair, ran out of the room and into the hallway. He bounded up the stairs two at a time and ran to his daughter's bedroom. His heart thumping, his breath coming in short bursts, his trembling hand turned the handle and slowly opened the door. He strained to see in the darkness, but as his eyes became accustomed to the low light, he saw that his daughter was sleeping peacefully in her bed.

Back in the living-room he looked around. The girl was gone. He felt a cold draught and going towards the kitchen he heard a sound like the bark of a dog, once, clear and sharp, then once again. In the kitchen the French windows were open, the sea beyond flat and calm and dark, with the moon emerging from behind the clouds. That is when he saw it in the water, the dark head glittering with wetness in the pale light. It was a large dog seal, looking towards the beach and it gave another single, loud bark. At once a higher-pitched, answering bark came from a cluster of rocks. That is when the man saw her, the strange girl, walking down onto the sand, her long ringlets, her white dress ruffled by the breeze. As she went, she appeared to be draping some kind of hooded cloak over her shoulders. She stepped into the water. The man wanted to shout, "No, no, what are you doing?" And yet so mesmerised was he by the scene that he could say and do nothing, but merely stood with his hands tightly clutching the door frame.

Slowly the girl waded into the sea, the dark cloak billowing behind her on the water until she pulled it tightly around her body and lifted the top over her head, which was all that was now showing as she swam out to the dog seal. He growled a greeting and this was answered by the girl. Then the two of them swam away from the beach and just before the moon went behind a cloud, the man seemed to see the heads of two seals, before they were gone into the depths below and he was left wondering if there had been anything there at all.

When his wife returned home two days later, he was so much in doubt about the reality of his experience that he told her what *appeared* to have happened. She was dismissive, saying that he must have fallen asleep and dreamt the whole thing. Over the next few days, he almost came to believe this himself and wondered why he had even mentioned the incident, which, at this remove, seemed more incredible than ever. However, on Christmas morning, as his daughter played with her presents from beneath the tree, the man saw that she was wearing a shell necklace, very similar to that worn by the strange girl. When he asked her where she got it, his daughter said that she had found it, wrapped in seaweed, amongst her presents. Her mother said that it had probably been dropped by one of her daughter's friends, but neither mother nor daughter seemed to make any effort to find out who that might have been. The man said nothing, though each time he thought about the incident, he had a hollow feeling in the pit of his stomach and the return of the faint memory that he had smelled that unusual odour somewhere else.

It was some months later when the man heard the tale of the newborn baby girl, wrapped in seaweed and wearing only a string of shells around her neck, being found outside the kitchen door of Rockport Lodge many years before. At the time, the locals had said that the child must have been left there by *an maighdeann-roin*, a seal-woman. It was certainly an interesting story but surely just another fairy tale, along with those about leprechauns and haunted houses, which had once been common in the Glens. The man smiled at his own naivety and told no-one else about his experience.

One day, in search of an old book, he went into one of the storerooms at the side of the house. Looking out of the window and across the sea, towards Garron Point in the distance, he suddenly smelled the strange, musky odour once again, stronger this time. Catching his breath, he turned quickly, his eyes raking over the boxes, the bags, the old furniture that almost filled the room. Then slowly he moved amongst them, head bent, sniffing here and there. Nothing. Until he came to the old cabin trunk.

It belonged to his wife, who had said that it contained mementoes of times past, of her first husband, of a lost child. He knelt on the floor beside it. Now the smell was even stronger. When he tried to lift the lid, he found that it was locked. He stared at it for a few moments and then decided. He had to find out what was in there. He jumped up and left the room, shortly returning with a screwdriver. The hasp on the lock came away quite easily and yet he paused before slowly opening the lid and being assaulted by the very strong odour. He grimaced and peered inside.

At first it was hard to distinguish what was in the trunk, but as he opened the lid wider, he could see that it was some kind of skin, dark grey mottled with a lighter tone, dry and bristly. He pulled at the topmost part and it lifted in one piece. There was no doubt about it. It was a small sealskin and underneath it was a larger one. There was nothing else in the trunk. Slowly he closed the lid and gazed out through the window.

When he told his wife what he had found, she was very angry, saying that he had no right to break open the trunk, that these things were her personal possessions. She refused to discuss the relevance of the sealskins and said that the matter was now closed. But in truth that was far from the case, for, somewhere in the middle of that night, he awoke to find his wife gone from their bed and heard the sighing of wind as through a half-open door. He arose and looked out of the window. A lemon moon was shimmering across the waters of the bay. Then, at the edge of the rocks in front of the house, he saw two figures hurrying towards the sea. One was his wife, holding a bundle of material and behind her she pulled their daughter Ursilla.

In one horrifying instant all was clear to the man, the strange girl, the necklace, the sealskins and the tale of *an maighdeann-roin*. He raced out of the room and almost flung himself down the stairs. Anything but his beloved Ursilla! Through the kitchen and out of the open back door he went, bounding across the path, the sharp stones stabbing blood from his bare feet. Now the two figures were at the edge of the water. His wife had pulled on what he now realised was the larger of the two sealskins and was wrapping the smaller one around Ursilla.

"No!" he screamed. "No, you can't do this! Ursilla, come back!"

Eyes wide, she turned to look at him. Her mother dragged her towards the lapping waves.

They entered the water as the man ran out onto the sand. It was then that he saw, a little further out, the head of a dog seal and another, smaller one nearby. The dog seal gave a sharp bark. Now mother and daughter were waist deep in the sea. The man sprinted across the sand and threw himself into the water after them. He swam as hard and as fast as he had ever done in his life. As he got to them, the water was up to their shoulders.

"Ursilla, no, no!" he screamed and reached out for her. The girl, staring-eyed, confused, turned to look at him. Her mother tried to pull her away. The dog seal barked. Then the man managed to grasp the shell necklace around his daughter's neck. He wrenched at it and as it broke and sank down through the dark water it was as though a key had been turned. Ursilla immediately pulled herself away from her mother's grasp and clung to her father. The woman, the mother, *an maighdeann-roin*, without a glance backwards, swam out to the other two seals. There were barked greetings before three seals slipped beneath the water.

On the beach, the man and his daughter stood clinging to each other, shivering and crying, their tears mingling with the beads of sea water on their cheeks, their faces glistening in the wan light of the moon. It was not many weeks before they left Rockport Lodge and found themselves a new home, many miles inland, far from the sea and those who live in it.

# La Llorona

*By Jess Allen*

They went when the day's heat started to dim. When the sun perched low above the tree line and the cicadas began their screaming song, when the stores lining the streets started to turn in their signs, when it was bearable to explore the ground with feet bare, that's when they went.

Past the town and its lingering patrons, past quiet suburbs and sprinklers waving, across the bridge and down to the river. As they left the town behind, the only sounds that followed were their tyres trawling through the high grass and the sound of TJ's broken chain; the three of them, every late afternoon that summer. Red, yellow, silver, one after the other.

On this day they sat by the riverbed. The day's heat had been immense; oppressive and exhausting, and there was not much to do now so late in the summer – they'd done it all. Movies, ice cream, bike tricks, climbing trees, catching fish - they'd fulfilled every list, every new idea gleaned from the TV to fill those endless days between school years.

It had been quiet between the three boys for some time when Mateo spoke:

'Do you guys want to go get burgers? I heard Mr. Namaya say after the dinner rush he was going to give leftovers out for free?' While he spoke, Mateo twirled blades of grass between and around his fingers with rough, bitten nails, the brittle stems crunching from that dry, dry summer.

There was a beat of silence. After all, there was no rush here. The water from the river whispered quietly to them for a moment before TJ said simply:

'Nah.'

TJ was tough for a twelve-year-old. Tough in the way that pit bulls were tough, or Dobermans were tough; they were trained that way. When Mateo would look back on these summer days, he would often wonder what TJ would have been like in another world, another circumstance. Although, as his mother would tell him, this wondering would never do any good.

Mateo sat up on his knees, picking another blade from the ground and bending it. 'Okay, well... wanna go get ice cream? Or we can go back to my house, my mom won't mind?'

Jake, the oldest of the three, looked up from trying to fix TJ's bike chain.

'Why do you want to leave so bad, Mateo? Are you okay?' Jake wiped a dirty hand across his forehead, pushing aside the hair that fell there.

Mateo avoided his friends's eyes, plucking another stem from the ground, then another.

'No, I'm fine, it's just boring here. Can we just go?'

'Mateo,' Jake again. His tone was reminiscent of the boys's third grade teacher Mrs. Winters. She'd never raised her voice, not once throughout the whole year. Not even when TJ had blown spit-balls across the room for an entire morning. 'What's wrong?' Jake continued.

Mateo hesitated, eyes resting on his bare knees, dusty from kneeling on the dry ground, 'I just heard some bad stuff about this place.'

Like a pit bull, TJ pounced on this, 'What are you scared of? There's nothing out here 'cept maybe a beaver. What, you scared it's gonna bite you on the ass?' He laughed, and the sound cut through the quiet air around them.

Blood rushed to Mateo's face. '*No*. I just...'

TJ's voice cut through again: 'Or what, you scared of a bat? No wait, a racoon? Scared it's gonna start eating you cause you smell like trash! Ha-ha!'

'Shut up!'

Mateo had always thought TJ had a laugh that stung, it picked and poked at you until you were red and raw like a bee sting.

'TJ.' Jake said, and just like how his voice reminded the other boys of Mrs Winters when he was being kind, he sounded even more like her now, 'Stop it.'

The younger boy bit back his laugh with a scowl, ripping handfuls of grass and weeds from where he sat.

'What is it, Mateo?'

Mateo sucked in a breath, letting his dark hair, longer than usual, fall over his forehead. 'Can we just go?'

'For god's sake, why are you being such a baby?' said TJ.

'What if la Llorona gets us?' Mateo muttered into his dusty t-shirt.

'La what? Who the hell is that?' TJ sneered. Mateo's head perked up and he took in the blank stares and furrowed brows of his friends.

'La Llorona?'

'Yarona?' The butchering of Mateo's accent rolled off his back like water, 'What's that, like the beer?'

'No,' The rush of the breeze across the river almost took Mateo's words with it, he spoke so quietly, 'she's a spirit. A ghost who walks along the river looking for her children that she lost,' Before TJ could make another comment, he'd continued, 'years and years ago, la Llorona found her husband with another woman. She was so angry she drowned her own children in the river - 'Mateo peeked up through the layer of dark hair and saw his friends were watching him, really listening. He tried not to feel happy about it. ' – *this* river. When she realised what she'd done, she drowned herself, too. When her spirit got to heaven, God spoke to her and said she could not enter until she found her children's bodies and buried them, but when she came back to Earth, she found out that their bodies had floated down the river. Now, she spends eternity looking for them. If she sees kids out here by the river at night, she might think you're hers and take you!'

There was a beat of silence between the boys, the only sound the slow murmur of the river current and the breeze lifting the leaves on the trees and the hairs on the backs of their necks.

Mateo hadn't realised that they'd been talking so long that the sun had fallen behind the trees and possibly further. There were no streetlights out here by the river. Mateo shivered, and finally TJ spat: 'That's the dumbest thing I ever heard.'

Mateo glanced at Jake, whose arms were folded over his chest, shoulders hunched. His fingers tapped silent rhythms on his arms.

'It's true. My mom heard her crying before. She says the further away she sounds, the closer she is.'

TJ made that 'pfft' sound of disbelief that brought all the blood to Mateo's olive cheeks.

'That's so stupid,' said TJ, 'I can't believe you ever fell for that. Afraid of something that ain't even there. I bet your mom just told you that so you'd always be back before dark, like a baby!'

'TJ,' Jake said. TJ's eyes flashed cold and blue.

'What? He's being a complete wuss! If you want to run home to your mommy, Mateo, go ahead. I'm stayin'. I'll stay here all night, I ain't afraid.'

'Oh yeah? Well, have fun out here with no friends, asshole!' The last word felt foreign on Mateo's tongue, the way his mother's Spanish sometimes did. It left a stale taste in his mouth.

'Guys…,' Jake said quietly.

'Fine by me! You're twelve now, Mateo, but sometimes you act like you're two! So run home, isn't it your bedtime anyways?'

'Guys-' Jake again, louder this time.

'No, you know what? You're just more scared of going home than being out here. Who's the baby now?'

'*Guys.*'

When they looked at Jake it was as though they were looking at someone else entirely. Jake was many things, but he was never afraid, and that was what they saw in him now.

And that's when they heard it.

Over the hushing sound of the river, over the insects humming in the grass, they heard it. Like a song, a wail, a cry that carried over the trees, raised the skin on the backs of their arms.

'Run!' Mateo shouted and was on his bike in a second, peddling away as fast as his legs would take him, the other boys just inches behind.

Over the creak of the peddles, the crunching of TJ's chain and their own thumping hearts, they could no longer hear the wailing. It only made them pedal faster.

When they reached the edge of town, TJ split off at the intersection as usual towards his family's apartment on the other side of the hill. Then, 2 minutes later, Jake veered off towards his street, not looking back. They'd ridden back in silence, save for their wheezing breaths.

When he arrived home, Mateo threw his bike into the back yard, ran through the front door and locked it behind him, resting his back against it to slow his heart. The house smelled of his mother's cooking, and he could hear her singing in the kitchen. He checked the door was locked once, twice, three times, then made his way to his room. He was home. He was safe.

When TJ arrived home, he did not feel safe. The third-floor apartment his family occupied was dim, the only noise came from the old TV but even that was loud, erratic.

It was almost ten o'clock. The young boy hoped he could escape to his room unnoticed and wish away the fear that had followed him from the river. But when he closed the front door it made a small 'click', and he flinched.

A rustle from the living room, the thud of a bottle on the table, then a loud voice like a bark. TJ thought that even the cry of la Llorona was a sweeter sound than that.

'Kid!'

He sucked in a breath through his teeth, and went in.

When Mateo awoke the next morning, it was as though the seasons had changed overnight. The scorching heat from the days before had given way to a chill that struck Mateo through his open bedroom window, and the sky outside was grey and heavy.

He'd slept soundly, the words of his mother having lulled him into comfort before bed. She'd listened to his fearful recount of the evening with a sad smile, told him she was glad he was back safely and had left the hall light on until he fell asleep. He'd never admit it to his friends, but Mateo loved his mother dearly. So, when she woke him up in the morning looking so troubled, it panicked him.

'Mami? What's wrong?' It usually made her smile to hear him speak more Spanish. It did not make her smile today. She sat at the edge of his bed, hand on his.

'Honey... when did you last see TJ yesterday?'

Mateo blinked, picked at the frayed edge of his bed

sheet, 'Um, after we biked back to town. He went home the same way as normal, up the hill?' He wanted to ask *Why*? but was too afraid.

And he had been right to be afraid. When his mother told him what had happened, it was everything he could have been afraid of and more. It did not feel real. It was as though she was speaking words from the TV, words that he heard but were not connected to him. They couldn't be connected to him, because things like this didn't happen, not to him, not to his friends.


It took many weeks for Mateo to return to the river. By that time, the leaves on the trees were browning at the edges and school had started again. 7th grade didn't feel right with one of their trio missing. Every day, Mateo and Jake waited just a few seconds at the intersection on the way to school but, of course, no one met them there.

The river itself was just as calm, just as careless as ever. Mateo stood and looked out across the river's edge, hands in his pockets and breathed: in and out; in and out.

When he heard the noise, it was loud, and it was close. It was a cry; a wail that he felt deep in his stomach, made his fingers numb with fear. His breathing stopped. The cry grew louder, like the scraping of teeth, like ringing in your ears, it was unbearable. For a moment, Mateo's chest grew tight and he felt that weight, that aching soreness of something missing that would never come back. That cry was this, this feeling. It built up and up on the inside of him until he thought he couldn't take it anymore. He pictured the face of the grieving woman in his mother's story, and he felt for her. Maybe, he thought, if he saw her, he would tell her that he understood.

And then, out of the trees, a bird.

A white bird, big as a plane on the backdrop of the

evening sky. Opening and closing its mouth, releasing the sound he had been dreaming of every night since the end of that summer. It circled the tree line, blurring into the grey of the evening until its cries died out.

It was just a bird.

That evening, he stayed by the river alone until dark, until the chill of the night pushed his hands further into his pockets and urged him home.

# The Second House

*By N G F Clark*

The witch strode in, her gaze drawn to the small tray of colourful mints sitting on my desk. Her teeth glittered like a set of carving knives.

I motioned her to sit and waved away her guards. The witch's pale arms were snaked with veins like two marble cenotaphs, ivy choked. I could smell her from here, a musty, back-of-the-spice-cupboard stench.

Prison did not suit her. Solitary, rural, and ancient, the witch could chant every name, could chart the rise and fall of the tiniest mayfly that shared the small space she called home. But the moment she strayed from that intimate *Umwelt* she was as gormless as a landed trout. I wanted to sink my teeth into her.

She made a display of discomfort as she slid onto the couch, as if it were the first time, she had lain down in all her long life. Her eyeballs rolled in their sockets like humbugs on a corner shop counter.

There was a knock at the door and my secretary scuttled in, clutching a parcel.

'Your post–'

'Not now, Margaret, I have a patient.'

'But you wanted to know–'

'*Just* leave it.' She bobbed back out, dropping the parcel in the in-tray as she went. The witch watched her retreat through lidded eyes.

I let the ceiling fan fold in the renewed silence of the room. Appetite is anticipation. 'Do you want to tell me what happened?'

'Why?' she snapped. 'Everyone knows. The whole

world knows. I could visit the bookshop in the next street and buy you the published court transcript, abridged,' she added, with a glitter of her pink and green iris.

*Strawberry and mint*, I thought. Out loud, I said: 'Very well. Would you like to tell me why things happened the way they did?'

The witch challenged me with a bored tilt of her head. 'Isn't that your job?'

The case had been drip-fed to me, filtered through layers of secrecy, and even with all the public clamour there remained something hidden from view. Despite my repeated demands for openness, I had been met with excuses and lies: lay-offs, extended absences, concerns of public security – a smokescreen of nonsense.

In the meantime, I had read and re-read the case obsessively, noting the careful obfuscations in each release from the authorities. I had shut down other cases, other patients, despite the reputational damage. It didn't matter. I had to know. And now here she was – plump, plucked and trussed.

'Let's start with you then – tell me about your parents.'

'Ha! I learned all I know from my mother; my father was present for my conception and retired from service shortly after.'

'Did you learn your cookery skills from your mother?'

She gave me the sort of look that, in a less civilised time, would have sent me scurrying to the local Justice of the Peace for fear of *maleficium*. But I weathered it and was rewarded with a glimpse – beneath that bubbling contempt – of a long-suffered loneliness.

'When did you discover you were capable of gastronomancy?'

The witch tutted. 'You like to put things in boxes, don't you? Neat little cabinets with brass frames for courier-typed numbers. But that's not how things work.'

More weathering, and after a while she huffed.

'I suppose I won't be allowed back to my concrete shoebox unless I convince you to convince *them* we've made some progress today?'

I swallowed a smile and dabbed at my lips.

After a while, she said: 'Like all things you put in the time. You watch the best, you imitate the masters, and after ten thousand hours you become a master. And people respect you. And after a hundred thousand, you become a magician. And people fear you. At some point you cross a boundary where your ability to do things is perceived as beyond what is normal.' She shrugged. 'Since it is no concern of mine, I let other people decide that.'

I wasn't sure if she was teasing me with her indulgent take on pop psychology. Either way, I enjoyed it. "What caused you to leave?"

'I continued in my apprenticeship until I outgrew it; after it became clear to me that there were too many chefs, to emasculate a phrase. So, I left. I have not seen my mother since, although I hear she is doing well.'

My ears pricked at her last remark, but the barbed follow-up never came – her gaze had settled to an intense contemplation of my spider plant.

From my drawer I pulled out a glossy Sunday supplement. A marble-eyed woman – prim, sharp, self-assured – stared out from the cover. Despite the bizarre reversal of appearance between the woman on the cover – who looked in her early forties – and the wrinkled old dame on the couch before me, there was a strong family resemblance. Or perhaps it was that same stare, a cool intensity from centuries of practice.

I flicked to the centre-spread and read aloud the headline: 'Top Culinary Witch Says of Cannibal Daughter

– "She Is Dead to Me"'.

The witch exploded with a snort; 'Old news!'

I read on: 'Celebrity food conjuror and headmistress of leading school of gastronomancy breaks silence following conviction of daughter in cannibalistic murder of two children, both of whom she lured onto her premises–'

'Yada yada,' mocked the witch, 'sensationalised baloney.'

'The facts are there,' I said over my spectacles, 'but we both know there is more behind the tabloid headlines.'

She looked at me oddly. 'Do you?'

I did my best to hide the flicker of uncertainty, but she caught it and her smile broadened. 'You don't, do you?'

'Were you aware your mother had achieved such prominence in her craft and industry?' I continued abruptly, decrying my heavy-handedness.

'You haven't seen it yet. *They haven't shown you.*'

I ignored her, scribbling nonsense in my notepad until I had shaken off the sudden pall cast in my mind. I pulled myself together and went on the offensive.

'You didn't leave your mother's academy, did you? You were kicked out. You were good, I have no doubt, but not good enough to be the daughter of the world's leading practitioner of food conjuring.'

The witch chuckled softly.

'I was her child – and yet she still counted me as an equal amongst those fawning students, those talentless toadies. From the day my apprenticeship started, I was reduced to just another name in the register.

'That school of hers was never anything more than a cult. She didn't just demand excellence from her students, she demanded *worship*. And what self-respecting teenager worships their mother? Having a daughter embarrassed her – she had a mystique to maintain, and I was her foil.

Perhaps she would have kicked me out soon enough, but I didn't last that long. I couldn't watch the soulless procession of middle-grade sycophants any longer.

'Well,' she concluded, 'are you ready to diagnose me?'

I digested her theatre confession; she was enjoying skirting the point, knowing I couldn't see it. I picked up one of the mints from the tray and unwrapped the green-and-pink striped orb, popping it into my mouth. A sourness I had not noticed before intensified the more I sucked on it. I felt angry.

'Very well: You wanted to make your mother proud,' I accused her. 'You wanted to say, "look where I am now." You're nothing more than a disinherited attention-seeker, long nurtured by solitude and petty self-righteousness. Your callous *cri-de-coeur* could have been avoided if only you'd had some friends.'

The witch heaved out sandpaper-dry cackles, shaking like a jelly. She clapped her hands until she calmed down.

'Dull, aren't I? Here–', she pointed to her mother's image on the cover of the magazine, '- *that* is who you should be interviewing. Have you not wondered why the same personality adorns your cookery books, fronts your TV shows, shapes your buying habits, your nutrient intake? One by one they came before her: princes, governments, corporations – century after century, making their pacts. She bent to their whims, and in return she gained power. She thought she could have everything – long life, long youth. But now she is trapped in her cycle of mediocrity – she will never be fulfilled.'

'Do you feel fulfilled?'

'I learned the lesson my mother was too proud to recognise. To create something truly worthwhile, something that will outlast you, you need to give of yourself more than you take. You empty the best of yourself into your work so that by the end of it, you are nothing more than a hollow wreck, a mere witness to your creation.'

'So,' she cocked her head. 'Ask me what the house means.'

I stared at her, troubled by her display of sincerity. 'What do you mean by that?'

She snorted. 'Everyone wants to know the little girl's story, the little boy's story. The irresponsible parents. Everyone wants to know what happened in the woods and what I did. But no one asks about the house itself. So go on.'

I thought back on the censored reports, the withheld details, the impression of an absence being circled. Out of the corner of my eye I glimpsed the government package waiting in my in-tray.

'It was a literalised sugar trap,' I said, 'an impressive but ultimately excessive artifice of your ego – and in incredibly bad taste, I might add.'

The witch wagged her finger at me, and I capitulated: 'What does the house mean?'

The witch's eyeballs rolled in my direction. 'To live is to eat. Over and over: life, death, consume, life, death, consume. One eats to live and the other dies to be eaten. But who is the one and who is the other? The stories are told by those who get to eat first, they who decide what is right to eat and what is not. Those who do otherwise must be punished. The stories are lies: there is no morality of feeding, only that we should feed well.'

I frowned. There was a light in her eyes that told me this was not a riddle for riddle's sake. 'You killed and ate two children – this is not some distasteful metaphor; it is psychopathic murder.'

'You want to consume me. Since I walked into this room you have longed to devour me. Do you begin to see

your hypocrisy? Look at you, you are a wolf walking –
all men are wolves – have you forgotten? Soon you will
remember.'

'The only cannibal in this room is the convicted one
sitting before me; how do you explain your hunger?'

'All women are witches, all are daughters of Saturn.
As we age beyond normal lifespans, our appetites merely
become stranger.'

I decided enough was enough. 'You lured two children
into your home. You killed them. You skinned them. You
ate them. Why?'

The witch sighed. 'You have read the case. I have
always denied the accusation of cannibalism – it is just
another story of the one to show how the other eats
wrongly. The children I gave to the house - yes, every meat
has its place. Even their father could see that, he admired it
for so long.'

'And you did nothing to stop him leaving, after he
found you. So, you would get caught. So that in the ensuing
outrage you could let your mother know the depredations
you had fallen to – all to destroy her public image? A high
price for petty vengeance.'

The witch touched her temples, suddenly weary. 'You
are still ignoring the house. How can you understand
without seeing it? But soon everyone will.'

'The house was destroyed – what was left of it is laid
out on slabs; I've seen it myself.' I held up a print of a
photo I had taken when visiting the evidence display of the
gingerbread house – its curlicues of sugar craft still intact,
still remarkable.

She didn't even look at it. She said: 'Not that one. The
other one. The one they are hiding from you.'

I felt cold and my hands were trembling slightly. I called
my secretary to permit the guards back in and the witch

was escorted from my office without another word between us. I would not see her again.

The ceiling fan hollowed out the air of the room as I stared at the compressed leather of the couch that still bore the witch's shape. Then I remembered the parcel waiting in my in-tray.

It was a plain stiffened envelope. I ripped it open, spilling out its contents onto my desk. I sat down and flicked through the sheaf of field notes that lay on top – brief and technical, for the most part, but now and then a strange description caught my eye:

*It will not rot.*

*Other animals dare not go near it. There is an absence of ecology within a half-mile radius. At its centre, the lugubrious structure sweats, sits, shivers.*

*At night we can hear it settle in on itself. At present we are unsure whether parts of it are still alive.*

My attention shifted to the matte-finished photos.

The prints showed a building, at first glance a painting of an alpine chalet, smudged in oils. Except it was not a painting. It was a photo of a house – a house made entirely of flesh.

Meat entwined in strange meldings – bone and fat traced intricate mosaics across the walls in a chimeric ossuary. Gelatine-spun windows glistened with rainbow oils. Hooved joints criss-crossed the apex of the rooftop. In the hallway, a splayed ribcage supported a streaked ceiling of shank and haunch; marbled pillars of fat-lined tenderloin eased through the fish head floor.

(In the walls, the deboned forms of two children are hung, stretched like trophies, smiles as wide as a drum).

I tried to put them side by side, but the cumulative effect was too much. There were no photos of the interior other than what the photographer had taken through the doorway.

I wondered – is it a house? Or a shrine? I could not shake the sense of something Biblical, this tabernacle of flesh. It is an offering perhaps, to be burned (to please which god?) or an altar (to offer of what?), or both at once (yes).

I identified longer notes more recognisable as journal entries; skipping through the text lines leapt out at me:

*Jackson and Emir had both been quiet all day, not speaking to anyone, or each other. We avoided discussing the wet warmth that emanates from inside the house, or the feeling that we were being watched. None of us argued when Jared decided to shift camp out of sight of its walls.*

*When I returned from the village, Jared was already packing, his eyes lit with a panic that I could not diffuse.*

*They had left their equipment, their phones, everything. Jared had seen them entering the house, both naked. He had been too scared to call out to them. They have not come out.*

*I am leaving. It has been two days since Jackson and Emir entered the house. They have not come out. I am leaving.* An idea occurred to me. It is an ark - an inverted ark made of all species, butchered two by two.

I realised how inadequate my tools of analysis were in examining the mind that had built it. *Built* – such a flimsy label, behind which a void of understanding gapes. Language fails.

Perhaps the house is beyond even her now, perhaps it is beyond us all.

My thoughts became overwhelmed with a sense that she was still here, watching me. But when I looked up all I saw were the sweets inside their wrappers. I knocked over my chair and threw the tray across the room. As I stumbled to leave the office the prints slipped from the desktop, flopping to the carpet – *slop, slop, slop*.

'You look a bit wan, Mr W. Here, have a sweetie.' My secretary offered me the packet of pick 'n' mix she had been working through. Inside, children of all races and colours lay embalmed in sugar.

'Are you alright, sir? You don't look too good…'

She looked up at me through eyes of pink and green. I gagged and fled – I needed to get home.

Outside, the world had changed. Everyone I passed I viewed with suspicion. I had not taken the bus in years, but I needed something real and mundane. On the floor of the bus shelter was the bottom jaw of a penny sweet – red gums dusty with street grime, teeth still pointing upwards, as if half-bitten through the concrete. I tore my gaze away from it. As a bus passed by, I caught my reflection in its windows. A distortion in the glass elongated my face into a pointed muzzle and I retched with fear.It is now days later. I have barricaded myself in my apartment and have no contact with the outside. Society is turning in on itself as the influence of the witch house spreads. It happened from the top down, the dark heart of establishment devouring itself from the inside like a spreading cancer. I have not turned on the TV in days.

I am obsessed with watching the sun track across the sky. That huge orb of flame, consuming millions of tons of gas every second – the reach of its hunger blinds me. One day, like Saturn, our father the sun will remember us and return to devour us all, his carbon children, and all that we have failed to be.

I curl up on the floor and chew at my skin. I fear what I will become. A pit of hunger gnaws in my belly, growing every day, crowding out my thoughts. Already I have forgotten my name. Is this the flood that is coming? Its waters were here all along, now they swell from deep within us.

I will travel to the witch house. I will give myself to its walls.

# Madeline & the Door

*By Bethany Rainbird*

Madeline stood on the edge of the rock, taking a quick glug of her flask as she observed the other Seal Scouts. Some were distracted by the dismal grey waves, whilst others poked and prodded each other. Then there were the ones who hadn't been paying attention to the safety instructions — one in particular raised a clammy hand, his sleeves crusted with snot.

'What if our mapth go mithing?' he said with a lisp, his tongue pressed against his teeth. Madeline laughed from her perch, disappointed that the Scoutmaster's exasperated reply was just out of earshot.

With a dismissive wave from the Scoutmaster, the children began to shuffle along the shore, splaying maps and compasses on the sand. It wasn't long before a rather rotund Seal Scout found himself headfirst in a rock pool, emerging with a limpet branded to his forehead. The Scoutmaster's eye twitched, throwing a palm into her face with an expression that uttered 'I am *never* having kids.'

How hard can it be? Madeline thought with a frown. It's just reading a map! All she needed to know was to avoid the Door, or else she'd be taken — and promptly eaten — by the Locksmith. That was it.

Tugging on her backpack and pushing her spectacles up her nose, Madeline scampered to her first destination. Past the fishmonger's at the edge of the dock, then along the sailmaker's on the shoreline, and towards the top of the great looming cliffs. Emerging onto a dirt track, she consulted her map. It was often used by goat herders; their pastures marked out with battered stoke fences and prickly hedges. Madeline frowned. The track, despite being marked as a single lane, instead forked into two separate paths.

Then, from behind, the once-distant bellowing from cows was suddenly right behind her. Madeline stepped aside, allowing them to shuffle past.

'Can *you* tell me where to go?' she asked one of them sarcastically. 'Suppose all you know how to do is eat grass all day and be turned into beef,' she muttered. Just as the words left her mouth, her map seemed to have left her hands, too. Now, it belonged to the cow's stomach. 'Hey!' she yelled, the rest of the cows sweeping her into the herd. 'Give that back!' Madeline kicked and pushed — unable to fight against the bovine torrent. She looked ahead, an open door in the wall of the cliff. *The* Door. 'Oh no! Let me *go*!' Wincing, the cows pushed her forwards and past the threshold, disappearing with a final wail: 'I don't want to be eaten!'

Madeline groaned as she pushed herself off the ground, eyes darting around the cavern — not a single cow to be seen. Columns of sunlight filtered through gaps in the ceiling, cold water dripping from the stalactites and down onto her raincoat. Behind her, the Door was closed, its battered frame secured into the wall. What was most peculiar, however, was that the cave bore a striking resemblance to the cliff on the other side.

She tugged the door handle. And tugged again.

'Gah!' Madeline heaved, tumbling back into the dirt. With a whimper, she dusted off her raincoat, eyes stinging. Shaking her head, she leapt to her feet and recited: 'A Seal Scout should never give up!' Nodding determinedly, she headed towards the exit of the cave.

She gasped. The pastures, fences, and hedgerows were gone. Instead, a great forest travelled down the cliff, across the shore, and past the non-existent fishmonger's. Its leaves breathed with the breeze, swaying with a pleasant whisper. There were trees Madeline didn't even recognize — their trunks blushing under the glow of the golden sun. In the distance, the shadows of soft clouds cruised over the lush hills, grass blooming with a vibrant spectrum of flowers.

'This wasn't on the map,' she gulped, scanning the tree line. 'Oh!' Madeline quickly saluted, the glimpse of a magpie's head peeking out from behind a bush. She didn't want bad luck, of course. 'Hello Mister Magpie, how's your wife and family?'

'Quite well, thank you,' it replied, turning to face her. What Madeline hadn't noticed was that beneath its rather normal magpie head, was the body of a man — and a dapper one at that. Dressed in a pristine suit, his gloved hands clutched a top hat and cane. 'Oh crumbs,' his beady eyes widened, suppressing the need for much stronger language. 'Don't tell me you're from the beyond the Door?'

Madeline's mouth fell agape.

'How rude of me, allow me to introduce myself.' He bowed with a tip of his hat. 'I am Viscount Maguire Piecroft von Sandalwood.' She blinked, unsure of how to respond.

'Y-you're a bird!'

'Well observed!' he said, offering a hand. 'It appears you're a human. You must have a name. What do they call you?'

'Madeline,' she uttered hesitantly, adjusting her spectacles as if it would make him any less of a magpie. 'Those stupid cows,' she cursed, 'they stole my map!'

'Those rapscallions,' he frowned as much as a bird could. 'They have a taste for mischief, you know.'

'Cows?' Madeline recalled their bulky frames and dopey eyes, finding it quite difficult to believe.

'Oh yes,' he shook his feathered head. 'Quite the troublemakers! I say, perhaps you need some assistance in finding this map of yours?'

'It's no use!' Madeline said, stomping in her boots. 'I can't open the Door— I can't get back! I'm going to be in so much trouble. More than usual. What if the Locksmith finds out?'

'The Locksmith?'

'He'll eat me! I'll go missing — and nobody will find me!'

'My, how unpleasant,' he blinked. 'I suppose you had better get back before this Locksmith finds you, then?' She nodded apprehensively, wondering whether a talking bird still fit the bill of stranger danger.

'Wait...*you* won't eat me, will you?'

'I was about to ask you the very same question,' he said, stepping into the forest. He paused, tilting his head: 'Come along now, a dear friend of mine may be able to help.' Madeline took a deep breath and, with a final glance at the cave, followed the Viscount.


'What's with all these trees?' Madeline asked. 'We don't have these where I'm from.' She singled out a tree of iridescent bark. 'What's that one?'

'Araucarioxylon arizonicum: the rainbow wood,' he replied. 'Extinct where you live, I believe. But here, they're important for our ecosystem. Otherwise, we may not be around for much longer.'

'Well, why don't you tell the ecosystem that I'm the Seal Scout tree-planter world record holder,' she said triumphantly. 'I once planted four trees in a day.'

'Why not make it five?' he smiled. 'If you managed that, perhaps you'd have a forest like this, too.'

'But we need that space for houses and farms.'

'We seem to manage just fine.'

The Viscount gestured ahead to the forest opening into a glade. In the centre perched a crooked cabin, patches of moss sloughing off the wood and pearlescent smoke billowing from the colourfully stained chimney. The Viscount pushed open the front door.

'Professor?' he called. Madeline shuffled in after, her boots squeaking with every step. The interior was as neglected as the outside — bookshelves and ugly armchairs coated in a thick layer of dust.

'Maguire, is that you? It's about time you showed up,' said a nasal voice from the other room.

'Snarchimedes, always a pleasure.'

Madeline couldn't help but gasp — Snarchimedes was indeed a sight to behold, with the body of a man and head of a snail. He seemed to notice her at the same time, dropping his stack of books with a gasp.

'A human!' Snarchimedes exclaimed, collecting the books from the floor. 'Maguire, what have you done now?'

'Well, Madeline here seems to have had a run-in with those rambunctious cows,' he began. 'If you don't mind, she could do with a map of her home.'

'You think I have that kind of forbidden science lying around here?' The Viscount nodded firmly. 'Hmph, fine. I suppose I have the odd map lying around.' Approaching a bookshelf, he tugged on one of the books. Suddenly, the wall swung open, revealing a hidden room.

Hundreds, if not thousands of maps, lined the walls. Some sat on mangled stools scattered across the room, whilst others simply found themselves on the floor, incomplete and tarnished with footprints. In the centre of the room was a large table stained with ink and charcoal.

'These are all other worlds?' Madeline gasped, desperately scanning the different maps.

'Quick, Maguire. Fetch me some paper before the girl gets curious — well, *curiouser*.' Snarchimedes shoved a pot into Madeline's hands, ink splashing her coat. 'Make yourself useful.'

'Have you ever been to my world?' she asked, unsuccessfully trying to wipe the black stain from her coat.

'Why in the worlds would I ever do that?' He pulled a slab of wood from a shelf. 'That was Maguire's job. Now Queen Lynna's taken over, this kind of thing—' he gestured broadly to the maps '—is strictly banned.'

'Why?'

'Maybe you haven't noticed, but your world doesn't exactly take kindly to strange beings.'

'You're not *that* strange,' she said.

'I'm flattered,' he replied caustically, dropping the slab on the table with a thud. 'But I think that says something about you.'

Up close, Madeline could now see the familiar routes of her home engraved in the wood. With haste, Snarchimedes dipped a brush into the pot, slathering the grooves in ink, liquid pooling in the streets and roads. The Viscount placed down the paper as Snarchimedes flipped the slab over, and with a final press down, the map had taken shape.

'Don't lose this one,' he said, wiping slime from his brow. She gazed in awe, it was far more detailed — and accurate — than any map she had seen. 'Now, Maguire, I could really use your help with the new keys—'

'What better time, Professor?' he said. 'We have new keys *and* a human test subject,' he winked. 'Besides, we'd better return her before the Locksmith gets her.'

'The Locksmith?' he tilted his gooey head.

'A monster,' said Madeline. 'Anyone that gets too close to the Door goes missing. He *eats* them.'

'Is that so?' he looked to the Viscount. 'Suppose that

is more important.' Placing the pot of ink to the side, Snarchimedes reached for a satchel and slung it over his shoulder.

'You're coming with us?' Madeline asked.

'You could at least sound excited,' he said, following them out the door.

Stepping into the cave, Snarchimedes clutched a lantern, the flame casting skittering shadows against the wall. Bored, Madeline traipsed around outside, inspecting the trees. Meanwhile, the Viscount took position outside the mouth of the cave. Fiddling with a shimmering key, he remarked on the fresh hoofprints outside.

'I suspected those cows had found elsewhere for their gang.'

'About time they bothered someone else,' Snarchimedes yelled back. 'Still haven't forgiven them for ratting us out.'

'Language, Professor. You know how the rats feel about that term.'

'*Snitching* on us, then,' he corrected. 'Those cows should be thanking us. How else would they get to the human world?' He picked up the last key from the Viscount. 'Come to think of it, how *did* they get to the human world? We're the only ones with the keys.' The Viscount dodged his glance. 'Hold on, you've been exploring again, haven't you?'

'Well, you see-'

'Maguire!'

'Snarch!' The Viscount parroted, watching as Snarchimedes rolled his eyes and headed back to the Door. 'It was just a quick trip to try and check on those unflattering rumors. Nothing's changed, may I add! In fact, it seems it's gotten rather out of hand.'

'Do you have any idea what would have happened if

Lynna found out?'

Just as their focus wavered: a yelp from the trees.

'Let go of me!' Madeline cried. The Viscount leapt to his feet, feathers quivering as he turned to face the cry.

'Piecroft!' a voice screeched. He flinched.

'Oh *crumbs*.'

Marching over the hill was a woman with the head of a lynx. Her appearance was striking — a scar dividing the mottled fur on her face. On her head sat a polished silver crown, fashioned to resemble branches and leaves. She wasn't like any Queen Madeline had known; adorned with armour instead of a dress. Behind her stood a swarm of guards — ferrets, weasels, badgers. And Madeline. She snarled: 'I should have known this was your doing!'

'Lynna, your majesty,' the Viscount bowed halfheartedly. Just in time, Snarchimedes emerged from the cave, keys rattling in his hands.

'Of course! The slug's here too,' she said viciously.

'Great,' Snarchimedes sighed.

'First, you steal from the crown,' she said, taking a step towards the Viscount. 'Then, you steal back the keys.' Another step. 'Now, you steal a *human child*. I mean, have you gone completely mad? How did she get here?'

'Suppose she just… wandered in?' Snarchimedes shrugged. The Queen swiped him out of the way as if he were made of cotton. Then, with a rigid finger, she pointed at the Viscount.

'I thought I made it clear that any more meddling would land you in prison.'

'Oh yes, perfectly clear,' he said. 'But this seemed rather important.'

'We'd just like to send Madeline home,' said Snarchimedes.

'Yes, through the Door and on her way,' the Viscount

nodded.

'Those days of exploration are over,' she snapped. 'Guards!' Immediately, Snarchimedes and the Viscount found themselves seized. The guards looked at Madeline, unsure of what to do. A brave fox hesitantly grabbed her arm, flinching as she shook it off with a scowl.

'Stop!' demanded Madeline. 'Miss Lady Madame Queen Lynna,' she began, hoping at least one of the titles would be correct. 'If I may?'

'If you *must*,' she bared her teeth with a huff.

'Have you ever been to my world?'

'Don't waste my time with ridiculous questions. Make it quick.'

'In my world, we have the Locksmith,' Madeline said quickly. 'He's a monster and a thief. He'll take anyone caught messing around with the Door… then *eats* them.'

'Eats them? You humans are far more uncivilized than I thought.'

'In my country, lynxes went extinct a long time ago. I guess he liked their taste.'

'Piecroft, you know this world, is that true?'

'Of course,' he lied. 'I know the Locksmith *very* well, he has ample time on his hands. I'm sure he wouldn't mind paying a visit.'

'Worst of all, he's my friend,' she grinned wryly, trading a look with the Viscount— the Queen was gullible. 'Can't imagine what he'll do when he finds out about all this.'

'You're *friends* with this barbarian?' she gasped. 'You humans are truly terrible!'

'Wait, did you hear that?' Concealed behind her back, Madeline threw a stone. It landed in the cave with a knock… knock... *knock*.

'What was that?' One of the guards squealed, shuffling closer to his squad.

'Sounded like knocking to me,' said Snarchimedes, turning to the Viscount. 'Wasn't he on his way?'

'Uh oh,' Madeline smiled, 'I think he's hungry.' Flustered, the Queen glanced at her trembling guards, her eyes wide. The fox wasn't feeling so brave, after all. He was the first to scamper away, followed by the rest of the guards. And seconds later, the Queen followed suit.

'Come back here and protect me! You're all fired!' Her voice boomed through the valley as she ran after the wayward guards.

'Good thinking, kiddo,' said Snarchimedes, relieved to be released from their grip.

'Didn't get my Seal Scout Scary Story badge for nothing.'

'Just in time, too,' he pointed to the Door. It was open. A thin, shimmering veil swirled inside its frame, flashing familiar images of her world. The Viscount nodded with a bittersweet smile.

'Until we meet again,' he said.

'One last thing…' And with that, she threw her arms around them both. 'How am I meant to explain all this?' She hugged tightly.

'Maybe some things are better kept a secret,' the Viscount said, glancing towards the Door.

'Hurry now, before it closes.' Snarchimedes gently ushered. Madeline took a deep breath and, exchanging a final smile, stepped into the Door. Gone. The veil faded, leaving just the dancing flames of the lantern to light the cave.

'Are you… crying, Professor?' the Viscount peered at his friend's eyestalks, placing a reassuring hand on his shoulder. 'Sometimes it's hard to tell.'

'N-no!' he wiped his eyes. 'I'm just allergic to humans.' The Viscount shook his head with a smile.

'I told you those rumors were unflattering,' he said, flashing the set of keys. 'Why would I ever eat a human?' he scoffed. 'Though I must admit, the Locksmith *does* have a good ring to it.'

# Ash

*By Katherine Gutierrez*

The cats were named after the *Seven Kings of Hell*, which amused Perla because they were such nice cats. The breed name she had forgotten, they were cream and blue with high-pitched voices. They lived a charmed life in a spacious loft that took up an entire floor of a high-rise building, entry granted by a golden elevator, light granted by the ceiling-to-floor windows, culture granted by Franz Kline copies in gilded frames, the changing seasons by mosaic faux wood floors that could be heated or cooled by a mechanism in the linen closet. The loft was another world compared to where Perla lived, which was in her aunt's basement; a place that garden termites had twice made their home, where it wasn't unusual for chunks of rotting beam wood to be found in her hair when she woke up.

Her aunt was named Eunice, but had changed it to Rin Zara for her artistic career. She hadn't gotten along at all with Perla's mother, Neris, which gave her and Perla something in common. Perla had gone straight to her grandmother's house in Goudhurst when she arrived back in England after a failed nannying job in Italy, penniless and disillusioned with her childhood dreams. Her aunt had taken over the house since her grandmother's death and agreed to let Perla stay for a month or so. Perla had arrived when she was twenty-seven. She was now thirty, the house looked worse than it ever had, her aunt drank two Absolut Vodkas to their dregs every day and Perla's main income was earned as a cat butler.

The last part, Perla didn't mind. She had never been academically gifted or even ambitious. She had relied solely on her looks to secure an alliance with someone who could earn a decent living. She often complained to her aunt that her looks were part of the reason she was kicked out of her employer's house in Italy, that the mother of the family had despised her. She left out that she had been sleeping with the father of the family. She also left out the fact that the children had hated her and would run from her, screaming, calling her a 'Tato Two'. Tato was the name of their spadefoot toad who lived in a fifty-seven litre tank in the greenhouse and was infinitely more liked than Perla had been. In short, Perla was happy to be working with cats rather than kids, especially the Kings of Hell cats, who seemed to like her immensely.

When she had gone for her first and only interview for the cat butler position, the cat owner Marla Kranz-Pillbody, had commented on how the cats took to her. She had told Perla to call her 'Mmmkay' because her nephews did, but Perla was too embarrassed. She showed Perla the spare bedroom which was a stunning high-ceilinged corner room with a dimmer over a canopy bed that faced the converted mill that was overrun by explosions of gorse and fire-flecked cypress; 'whenever you want it' she had said. Perla wanted it all the time.

Marla Kranz-Pillbody was more of a cautionary tale than a real human being. She was an art distribution regulator and spent large chunks of time in Eastern Europe, standing in cold Polish churches making sure things were bubble-wrapped securely. She had no kids or partner, just the cats. 'Crazy cat lady' Perla's aunt had called her and Perla thought that she might be right, even though Marla seemed saner than most people. She was pathetic, though, Perla thought. The kind of person for whom nothing goes well.

In February, Marla was gone every other week and

Perla stayed in the beautiful corner room. They had a quiet and organized arrangement where Perla would arrive just after she knew Marla had left, collect the money for the last stay from the entry room table and she would leave twenty minutes before Marla would arrive. Apart from texting schedules, dates, delayed flight times and the odd thank you, Perla and Marla had very little to say to each other. Perla saw her job like she was stepping into Marla's skin. When Marla was gone, she might as well be her as far as the cats and the house was concerned. Perla liked to pretend all this belonged to her instead.

Perla arrived at Marla's apartment mid-February, on schedule for another overnight stay. By now, Marla should be on the motorway towards the city.

Perla had often wondered why, with so much international travel, Marla had settled in Goudhurst rather than somewhere like London. She could've at least found something closer to a main airport. It might have been to give the cats more space, she really loved those cats.

Perla entered the door code and took the elevator up to the third floor where a second code was needed. She was greeted by an audience, seven cats bundled up at her feet, meowing, purring and rustling against her.

'Hello Belphagor,' Perla said. 'Hello Asmodeus, hello Satan, hello Leviathan,' she waded her way over to the entry room table and dumped her bag down. 'Hello Mammon, hello Lucifer, hello Beelzebub.'

Lucifer jumped on the kitchen table to inspect the bag. Perla unzipped it to take out her mug. Marla kept a very expensive coffee machine, the kind that Perla had only ever seen in John Lewis displays. She also kept a rotating rack of syrups: salted caramel, hazelnut, vanilla bean, gingerbread. There was a singed smell in the air. Perla had noticed it when she entered and it was stronger in the kitchen, as if the toaster or the oven had recently been on.

To make sure she was alone, Perla called out: 'Marla!' Twice. She opened the bathroom door, which was ajar to find that it was empty.

Leviathan and Beelzebub ingratiated against her legs, expecting food, Satan was cleaning himself in the doorway and Mammon had found something interesting about the legs of the kitchen chair and was scratching at them whilst laying on his side. The cats generally followed Perla to every room, or else could be found at their food bowls or in their litter trays.

Perla left the coffee to drip and went to inspect the smell. She wondered if another apartment in the building was on fire, but if that was the case she should be able to hear a fire alarm. There should be some clouds of smoke outside.

The cats observed her as she went from room to room, opening doors. They watched her as she opened the door to Marla's room, which was less glamorous than the spare room, stacked with filing and plastic boxes. In the bedroom, Perla finally found Marla.

Marla's imprint was burned into the kitschy wallpaper, you could make out a head, sloping shoulders and a slight torso above two legs that were bent as if to flee. On the carpet was a pile of grey ash, an invisible smoke was curling particles of Marla's burnt person into the air.

The mysterious death of Marla Kranz-Pillbody resulted in some internet interest. After the police investigation and local story, a few crime YouTubers made an episode covering the case and  a larger newspaper got hold of it for an article. They asked Perla if she would come to London for an interview and she declined. They asked her to provide a comment via email instead and she declined.

Spontaneous human combustion was like something you would read about during a tour of a Victorian museum; a period in time where lots of strange and terrible things had happened for no reason.

'What can you do? Some things aren't supposed to be understood completely.' Perla's aunt had said. She had been selected for an exclusive artist's residency in Scotland and was trying to cut down her drinking to one vodka bottle a day, so now she was smoking incessantly.       'Do you want to take it up?' She had offered Perla. 'It'll calm your nerves.'

'It's bad for you.' Perla had responded.

'Everything enjoyable is bad for you.'

Perla's nerves were calm. After the initial shock of discovering the pile of ashes that Marla had become, she had been concerned mainly with the cats.

The cats had been shipped off to live with Marla's sister and nephews. Perla had received one email from the sister to say that thank you for taking care of the apartment and the cats for so long. She mentioned that they had changed the cats' names for the sake of the kids, that saying 'Satan' and 'Lucifer' over and over when dinner was ready had proved too frightening.

Perla couldn't get the smell of smoke off her of skin and hair. It was different from the smell of cigarette smoke or the smell from a log fire. The closest thing that Perla could associate the smell with was 'barbeque'.

As she tried to rid herself of the smell with astringent and heavily fragranced 'old lady' soap in the bath, she noticed that Marla was standing next to the bundle of decorative shells that hung in a net from the door. Marla looked the same as ever, except that her skin was ash-grey.

'You're dead.' Perla informed her.

Marla opened her mouth and ash fell from it, creating a small pile on the floor.

Perla continued asking Marla questions over the days and weeks that followed. Although Marla occasionally disappeared, Perla never truly felt alone. She smelled not only smoke but also Marla's understated perfume when she entered a room.

'I know you're there.' Perla would say and sometimes the window would rattle or an ornament would fall from the shelf.

Nighttime was better for Marla. During the day, she often appeared as just a head peering over the breakfast table as Perla ate cereal or just an arm through the door as Perla filled out job applications on her laptop. During the night, she could truly be herself and she would appear in different outfits. Some of the outfits were modern and fashionable, like zig-zag crop tops and black denim skirts and some were clearly from a bygone era and they were covered in mud-like stains.

'Where did you get those clothes?' Perla asked and Marla responded by howling and the room shook and filled with falling ash.

After a few months, Perla found a new job for a writing website and bought a new coffee machine with her first paycheck so that she wouldn't have to live on instant.

Marla wrapped herself like a pretzel around the new coffee machine, showing her appreciation. Perla would leave a cup of coffee in front of the shrine that she had built for Marla in her room. She didn't know what to put on a shrine, so she put newspaper clippings about Marla's death, stones and flowers from the garden and a few printed pictures of the cats that Perla kept on her phone. Marla seemed ambivalent about the shrine, but the coffee cup was always empty when Perla came back. Marla also liked spicy gingerbread biscuits, they would disappear regularly from plates with not a crumb left.

'Do you know why you died?' Perla had asked many times. 'Or how?'

Marla didn't like those kinds of questions and rebelled by drawing tunnelling circles on the windows and the mirrors with soot. She set fire to items in the house.

'I'm starting to think we're haunted.' Perla's aunt had joked after the third unexplained fire in the living room, this time a tissue box on the table. Perla's aunt was looking at Perla expectantly, waiting for her to own up.

'Maybe.' Perla said. Marla was hanging upside down like a bat, mouth gaping, ash collecting in the sink.

Perla always made room for Marla in her bed. Marla took up a lot of space and Perla felt cold puffs of breath on her thighs as Marla curled up to sleep on her legs like a cat. When she looked underneath the blankets, Marla's face was on fire. When she closed her eyes, she felt the comforting sensation of Marla's head on her chest.

# Chimes

*By Brigitte de Valk*

The house smells faintly of oranges. The notion of bright, orbed fruit makes me smile. My fingers grip the handle of my suitcase, as I stand in the doorway. Blood blooms across my cheeks as I notice the trail of mud I have created with my boots.

I wait for the woman to return.

The oval mirror, hanging to my left, reflects the sharp, white points of my collar and a flutter of crimson as my smile widens. I am always practising my smile. I aim for naturalness in everything I do.

The woman returns.

I am led into a parlour. A grandfather clock looms in a corner.

*Tick-tock. Tick-tock.*

'I am the mother, of course,' she says. I look around for her child but he is not here. Brief touches of sunlight, slant from the tall windows, and spool on the wooden floor. Clouds indecisively shift across the sky. On her mantlepiece sits four silver bowls, filled with potpourri. She dips a hand into a bowl. I hear the rustle of dried petals and watch her bow her head to sniff.

'Fragrance is everything,' she frowns.

The sea is not too far away. I am eager to view its dark, cobalt dances. It's been so long since I have seen vast expanses of water. I try to ask her about the direction of the waves, but she turns her head away. She stares into an empty fire grate. Ash lingers on the cool tiles beneath. I put down my suitcase. A dull thud echoes around the room. The mother stiffens and then shows me to my room.

I am alone and yet I can still hear the grandfather clock. *Tick-tock. Tick-tock.*

I sit at my new desk and lay out my utensils. I trace a finger along burly pens, slender pencils and dishevelled paintbrushes. This is my new home. It seems as though I have already forgotten my train journey to the countryside. The tracks running behind me have been chopped up for kindling. The views from the window, that I stared out of for hours, have become muddled. I am here now, and a small lamp illuminates the dusty corners.

Night falls swiftly.

*Tick-tock, tick-tock, goes the blanched face of the moon.*

Three eggcups squat on the kitchen table. They are prim, brightly painted things. The mother sits opposite me, cutting her toast into pieces. I pick up a decanter of orange juice, and stare into its crystal inlay. All alcohol has been removed from the house. I slice off a pat of butter. The mother puts down her knife and stares at me.

'Magnolias upon magnolias, upon magnolias,' she smiles, glancing through the open back door. I twist in my seat, to see the thick boughs of a tree, reaching up towards the sky. Tight buds of the palest blush sleep in the morning mist. I hadn't noticed the tree yesterday.

I laugh, making sure my eyes crinkle in an authentic manner. The kettle emits a shrill whistle. Tart orange juice sears the soft lining of my throat.

The grandfather clock is fashioned from mahogany. I sit at a table with a stack of books and a pile of clean, white paper. My thin shirt clings to my skin. Its tiny, plastic buttons fall and rise with each breath. I lay an elbow against the wood. The skin of my cheek feels smooth. In my en-suite, a tiny pot of face cream, and a sliver of homemade soap perched on the sink. I had felt the urge to cradle them gently in my palms.

*Chimes sound sweetly.*

Another hour has passed.

The clopping of boots against floorboards grows louder. The mother enters the parlour in a daze. I sit a little straighter. I am expecting her son, who is late to our lesson, to appear behind her skirts. I have planned for arithmetic and perhaps a touch of poetry. I tell her that I'm ready. I smooth a strand of hair behind an ear, in casual affectation.

'Yes,' she says. She toys with her silk neckerchief and glances out the window. I mirror her. The sky is a volatile blue arching for miles, without a bird to be seen. Her reflection in the glass is beautiful. I open up a book. The mother leans over the table, and reads the numbers listed on the first page. She nods slowly.

*Tick-tock. Tick-tock.*

'My mind is so full of answers,' she reveals. 'At lunch we won't be eating beef.'

The rose hues of her skirt sway as she leaves the room. I quickly close the book. A drop of blood gathers at the edge of a papercut. I place the hurt finger on my tongue and shiver. A slight breeze intermingles with the dull air of the parlour.

Curtains billow, ghost-like and fragile in the cool night. My pen scratches against paper. Pleasure sprouts in my chest, freshly awakened. Ink stains the tips of my fingers. Lilting musical notes, drift upwards from the depths of the house.

Bombastic, blue, crashing. I am enlivened by the rough tide. Shadows linger under each knoll of water. Foam scatters along sand, wetting the tips of my shoes. I

am not needed today. The worksheets I had prepared, are
tucked away, in a locked drawer. Her son was not visible.
Pearlescent shells glint in upturned delight.

Coils of seaweed glitter. I traipse along the beach,
searching for pottery remnants and shattered sea glass.
I think of a painting, in which a woman finds a baby,
ensconced in a shell; an oyster so large, she could have
curled beneath it too. Gulls cry faintly.

My pockets rattle with stones, shot through with lines
of white and grey. My day unfolds slowly. The sea glances
at me, from time to time, its belly pure teal. The notion of
nakedness consumes me, and I want to toss off my clothes
and swim. People wander on the headland, tiny ants against
the glare of the clouds.

'Where is your son?' I want to ask. The mother is
nonchalant, and drapes herself along a windowsill, her
ankles crossed and lightly swinging. Her shoulders shrug
under a smart cotton suit. I have asked her instead, about
the time. She points to the grandfather clock.

*Tick-tock. Tick-tock.*

'Bleached by light,' she says. I peer at the dark wooden
grain of the grandfather clock. I secretly disagree. I
outwardly stare at the mother's face. Her large brow and
chiselled nose match the portraits in the hall, strangers
related by blood. She is distinctly tied to history and I am
afloat. My past is erased, by my own volition. I think of
painting my own profile, in a tiny two-inch frame, and
hanging it on the wall, partially hidden.

The floorboards creak as I shift from foot to foot. I hope
I will get paid, regardless of my empty days. The mother
sighs. Her coral nails scratch her nose. An opal ring weighs
down her left forefinger. The magnolia buds remain closed,
eyelids shut tight to the harried air.

I open my attic door. My room has been interfered with. My duvet is tousled and my pillow retains a deep imprint. Tubes of paint have been re-ordered, so that my cadmium yellows all wear different lids, and find themselves next to robust tones.

My sketchbook is flung open. A sentence has been scrawled in barely perceptible pencil.

*The numbers and the words, the numbness and the worlds, all spin delicately around, your mind.*

I rifle through my canvases, checking to see if the images, that bloomed from my paintbrush, are still intact. I pause at my rendition of the sea; its body muscular and translucent, beast-like, amoral. Cerulean. Nothing is amiss. I sit on a stool and touch the dark velvet of its padding. I am so private with my work. I would have never possessed the courage to show the mother what I laboured over in my spare time. Relief tingles gently across my body. I have been seen.

I pour myself a glass of water, from a jug by my bedside. I splash a little. Spring seems a little nearer, although it is dark outside, and I can not yet see the morning sun.

I think of the night as a field of soil, pitch-black and expectant.

The mother is wearing a wide brimmed hat and stirring cream into coffee. She is young to be a mother. It is as though she is de-aging before my eyes. Her teaspoon rings as she taps it against her enamel mug. I enter the kitchen, fully-dressed. I have started bathing before breakfast. I stare at my knees, below water, and the strange bruises which appear, haphazardly, on my shins. I pause at the sink. There is a mound of crockery to be cleaned. Orange juice waits patiently for me on the table. The mother has already gulped her orange juice down, orange swallow after orange swallow. Pith and debris linger on the rim of her cup.

Ivy creeps irregularly across the outside window ledge. I join the mother and sit in front of a polished plate. She discusses with me, the state of her raspberry conserves and the dates at which they will all expire.

'They hold special meanings for me,' she twists open a lid with a deft movement of her wrist. The air pops. A sweet aroma is released. 'Epiphanies in particular. The sensation of a new idea.' I nod, readjusting my shoulders, so they appear relaxed. The mother dips her teaspoon into the jam, staining the fuchsia jelly, with droplets of coffee. Seeds are scattered throughout the conserve.

The white contours of the magnolias are slowly easing open. She will, undoubtedly pluck their petals, dry them, and store them in hungry pots and jars and bowls.

Weeks hurry by. My room becomes an atelier. The grandfather clock, though elderly, provides a frequential dignity to the unused parlour.

*Tick-tock. Tick-tock.*

Pages flurry under my fingertips. Volumes perch on shelves like lost birds, until I find them. I caress their little egos by reading their contents. I no longer roam the house, looking for a child to teach. Days collect like shells in my pockets, I bring so many back to the house. I leave them scattered on the drive, under windowsills, on top of the piano. Sometimes I step on them and they shatter with an elegant crunch.

Sand particles grit under my nails.

One morning I awaken to the bright shock of daffodils. So many of them. Multiplying on the lawn.

# Approaching Terminus

*By Bhagath Subramanian*

There was a tunnel.

It was large, like the gaping mouth of some ancient world-eater. The size of the opening was so gargantuan, and the shape of it so eerie, that all who came upon it were overwhelmed by something that could not be described using any language that human tongues and throats could form the sounds for. If there was a way to grasp any idea of what it felt like, it would be to look upon the face of some shell-shocked soldier, or a shipwrecked sailor washed up on the coast, or the blank stare of a mother unable to process the death of her child.

He came upon it one day. His little rain boots were smeared with black mud and streaked with greasy soot. It was getting dark, and everything was so much bigger than he was. The creaking trees, the engulfing grey clouds, and even the leaves that managed to snap away from their branches seemed to be able to stretch across his face and smother him to death through intimidation alone.

But nothing was bigger than this. All of a sudden, the horizon was replaced by an endless black. It was there that the opening to the tunnel sat, wedged between mountain and mist- waiting. The valley spilled into the abyss. The ground rose to where the mouth was, and he could almost make out a slight dip downwards at where the lip was. There was a breeze. It was going into the tunnel. Everything converged at the mouth, flowing into it. Nothing was exempt. The trees continued, the bushes dotted, the mud and the slush and the dirt too. Even the air was compelled to enter the opening. He felt that if he waited long enough, he'd catch the ground itself shift and crawl, millimetre by millimetre, carrying the entire forest with it into whatever fate awaited all things in whatever place was beyond that dip, just past the lip.

He needed to see.

Slowly, he began to trudge through the slosh and grime. First, he felt the breeze at his back. It was cool, but nothing like he had felt before. It was air, formed into a guiding hand. Comforting, and icy.

Ever so faintly, there was a rustling- in the bushes, to his right. Before he could turn to look at the tree line, the deer had already darted out from it, and made its way to the mouth of the tunnel. It put one hoof over the edge, and soon the rest of it followed into nothing. It reminded him of some warm, dark, sacred place of silence. Of sleep.

He walked on. With every step, he noticed the colour draining. The leaves were grey, the sky was black. And the sound- everything was at a whisper. Soon, there was only silence, and all the light had been sucked out of this world. There was only enough to see the glint of the rim. He was at the mouth of the tunnel. There he was, faced with the unknowable weight of eternity careening over him. And he took the plunge.

They found his little body in a bright clearing. He was far from where they had made camp. He was cold. He had no more need for sleep.

# Shopping for Annie

*By Lesley Webb*

'Take a seat Madam,' the pharmacist said as he pulled an orange plastic chair away from the staffroom table and indicated to the woman to sit down. He focused his gaze on the Health and Safety at Work poster his predecessor had pinned on the notice board, it had turned brown with age and curled in places.

'*I should get that changed*,' he thought whilst also observing her from his side of the table. With her long red hair and green eyes, she looked like an Irish beauty, but her accent was that of a resident of a well-heeled London suburb.

'*Probably Kingston or Richmond.*' He noticed she was shaking as she spoke.

'I didn't see it coming.' I had not been trained back then, didn't understand how to duck and dive, or how to take it on the chin. So, Tim's fist connected with my cheek instead. Of course, it was my fault, I knew this was true because he told me.

'You stupid bitch! *Now* look what you've made me do.' He was cross with himself for stooping to my level. 'That was your fault.'

I couldn't blame him for my stupidity, could I?

He was so upset that he trembled and the blood drained from his face, which was odd because it flowed from mine.

'Here, let me clean you up. I'm so sorry I won't do that ever again, I promise.' He'd sobbed as he mopped my cheek with the first thing that came to his hand; a white and blue checked tea towel. I couldn't speak. He asked me if I wanted him to take me to the hospital, but I drove myself to the A and E department. When they cleaned the wound and put the sterile strips on, I gritted my teeth, in part so that I didn't have to answer their questions about how my cheek had exploded in slow motion on contact with my boyfriend's fist, like I had been in a movie or something.

I didn't break off the engagement because it had been my fault and I knew he would never do it again. My fiancée was true to his word he didn't do it again.

'You don't have to tell me anything,' Mr Patel explained wondering why on earth she was sharing so much with him. It seemed she wanted to talk none the less.

"The wedding was a bit of a disaster. We had planned a big do, but then a global pandemic kicked in and we had to change everything at the last minute. In the beginning we'd had a hundred guests on the guest list, then when the lockdown happened, we had to limit it to thirty and then a week before the big day we got another lockdown, and the guest list was reduced to just our parents and the best man. Fewer witnesses. I tried not to let it upset me, but it seemed wrong to plight my troth in front of so few people. I think it affected his perspective as well.

We had a meal after the ceremony – the hotel was registered to conduct weddings and then provide the wedding breakfast. Because it had all changed so much and in order to comply with lockdown, we had to make some adjustments to the menu. We couldn't have any champagne because they had changed the rules so alcohol couldn't be served with food anymore. So, no guests and no bridesmaids. No toasts and no speeches. Were we even married? I remember saying in sickness and in health till death us do part, but I hadn't understood the significance of those words at the time. I think they meant more to him than to me.

We didn't even have a photographer; the best man took the pictures on his phone. I asked him not to post them on social media, but he sent them out straight away before I'd had a chance to look at them. When I did see them, I couldn't find one picture that I was smiling in, not one. My forehead was crinkled in a frown in every picture. I must have been staring into the light or something.

Everyone left after the meal, they didn't want to stay late and get into trouble. I was sad because there was no dancing, I couldn't even throw my flowers at one of my friends. We went to our room and I thought we would just watch a film on television. He didn't think that was a good way to start married life. Funny really because I didn't think his idea was that good either. He'd had a bottle of champagne sent to the room and had started drinking some.

I don't know what the quarrel started over. I asked him which side of the bed he wanted to sleep on.

'I'm not planning to get much sleep, not on my wedding night,' he said. His voice was a bit peculiar when he said it. Like it had gone down a pitch or two. I laughed at first.

'Well, no, not at first but you're bound to want to go to sleep afterwards.'

Mr Patel shuffled uncomfortably on the orange plastic. He hoped it would deter the woman from continuing but she didn't notice his embarrassment.

I went into the bathroom to change out of my wedding dress and have a shower. When I went back into the bedroom the television was on, he'd selected a film, but it wasn't the sort of film I would watch. He'd found a porn channel. That would have to be paid for when we settled the bill.

'Do we have to watch porn on our wedding night?' I asked him.

'I thought it might give you some ideas,' he didn't switch it off.

'Please turn it off,' I said as I lay on the bed next to him and pulled the duvet over me.

'Are you a prude? Doesn't it turn you on?'

I started to explain that it didn't when suddenly he jumped on top of me, pinning my arms down with his knees. Then he slapped my face, on both cheeks.

'Get off me,' I shouted but he kept hitting me, then his slaps turned into punches.

I tried to push him off by heaving my body upwards, but he was much stronger than I was. Then I tried to scream but he put his hand over my mouth with one hand and his hand around my throat with the other. As wedding nights go, I wouldn't say it was what I'd imagined but I didn't have anything to compare it with. When I woke up, I crept into the bathroom and closed the door but there wasn't a lock. I looked in the mirror and hardly recognised myself. The skin around my eyes was black with mascara that'd run when I'd cried. My cheeks were red and puffy, but the scar hadn't burst open thank goodness. My neck had several purple bruises, the size of thumbprints.

'Do you need a glass of water?' Mr Patel enquired, as much to stop the flow of her story as anything else. His own mouth was dry.

'No,' she said then continued the grim tale. I wept as I dabbed a wet face cloth over my cheek. I thought *Oh God look at me*. I was about to run a bath when he came into the bathroom.

'Morning,' he said with a smile as he peed into the toilet bowl.

'I'm glad you didn't say Good Morning,' I replied.

'Oh, come on, don't be mad with me. I just got a bit excited that's all,'

'You could have killed me!' I shouted at him. I couldn't believe he thought what he'd done was down to excitement.

'If I'd wanted to kill you, I would have,' he said.

Then he put his arms around me and rubbed himself against me. My bath had to wait.

We couldn't go on our honeymoon because of the pandemic. I'd taken some time off work though and was glad because I had to wear a scarf around my neck, so that the bruises had time to heal. I've never told anyone about what had happened that night before.

She stared at the pharmacist. He nodded his head as if to encourage her, although what he wanted was for her to stop telling him her story.

'*I should've got one of the assistants to come in with her*,'he thought.

After a couple of weeks, I learned how to miss some of the punches. He thought it was a game and kept trying to catch me out. That was how he knocked me out, I think. I'd walked into the sitting room with a mug of coffee. I take my coffee black; he has milk.

'You forgot to put the milk in,' he said then he must have thrown a punch. The next thing I knew I woke up on the floor, my tee shirt was wet with coffee and my stomach was stinging from being burned with hot liquid. I think that was when I knew it wasn't going to change, that my husband wasn't the fiancée who'd promised not to do it again. My husband's promise was till death do us part.

'We've made the call: you can wait safely here in the staffroom Mrs…I'm sorry I didn't get your name.'

'I'm Natalie, Natalie Baker. Thank you. I can't take any more. That's why I came in today. I guessed he wouldn't stop me coming into a pharmacy. I told him I had to collect some feminine products – he doesn't like to hear about menstruation so I can't say I'm on my period or anything like that.'

The pharmacist couldn't help seeing bruises on the woman's wrist as she twisted her hands together one hand over the other, again and again. As he glanced at her face, he noticed she'd done a good job with concealer make-up on her scar.

'I heard that you could ask for help if you needed it. I couldn't phone a refuge or anything like that because he makes me hand over my phone to check the numbers I've rung. Since we've had lockdown, its worse because I can't get away from him when he isn't at work. He works shifts so I never know when he'll be out, he doesn't tell me which shift pattern he's on and even when he's not at work I never know where he is. He likes to surprise me by just turning up.'

The thought of her husband just turning up was a catalyst. Her composure crumpled, her shoulders shook, her face reddened, and profuse tears fell from her green eyes. The pharmacist was un-nerved. Caught between the embarrassment of trying to console the sobbing woman, and his anxiety at the growing number of customers waiting for their prescriptions to be fulfilled he couldn't help glancing at his watch.

'You don't have to worry, you're safe now Mrs Baker. Shall I get one of the assistants to sit with you?'

Trying to regain her composure she sniffed and wiped her hand across her cheek as if to dry the tears.

'Please don't leave me. I'm so frightened,' she whispered.

The pharmacist took a deep breath.

'I won't leave you till they get here don't worry. You were brave to come in and ask for help.'

'I heard about it on the radio. Just three letters they said. I thought it sounded like a girlfriend's name, you know Annie. When I took the tampons to the cash desk, I told the cashier that they were for my friend Annie. She didn't understand at first.'

The pharmacist made a mental note that he would need to train the staff to understand people might ask for help in lots of different ways.

'So, I tried to explain. My friend Annie has an unusual spelling of her name she spells it ANI. That was when the cashier understood and went to find you.'

'We are here for our community Mrs Baker, we're only too glad to help you.' He was about to say more when there was a gentle knock at the staffroom door. 'Come in.'

'Mr Patel, someone needs to speak to you about a lady called Annie.'

The pharmacist exhaled loud and long, grateful that he would be reprieved from the unwanted duty of listening to the poor woman's story. He could hand her over to the proper authorities.

'Thank you, Lisa, ask them to come in.'

A tall man stood in the doorway of the staffroom. He was only a couple of inches shorter than the doorframe itself. He wore a black padded waistcoat over a short-sleeved black shirt, the inner arm seams of which strained under the bulk of his biceps. In his left hand he held a peaked hat. Attached to his waistcoat was a small camera, which was filming. He didn't initially notice the woman as he addressed the pharmacist.

'Hello Mr Patel. I understand you have responded to an ANI distress call.'

'Hello Officer, yes thank you for coming so quickly. This lady is in need of help,' Mr Patel responded as he stood up, ready to take his leave of the situation that had taken up more than forty minutes of his morning. He turned to address her, confident that he'd done his duty. 'So, I'll leave you in the capable hands of this officer Mrs Baker.' Then he noticed. Natalie Baker was trembling. She looked like a balloon that had deflated.

'Mrs Baker, are you okay?'

She shook her head a little but said nothing. The pharmacist turned to the policeman. He noticed the man's right hand was clenched in a fist.

'Okay well I can take it from here. Shall we go?' Mr Patel heard the note of irritation in the officer's voice.

Natalie Baker stood up. She looked away as she walked past the pharmacist. A thin river of urine ran down her legs. A dark streak, which ended at her ankle, as if her tights were old fashioned seamed stockings but the seam had turned inwards. Her shoulders were down, and her footsteps dragged one in front of the other.

'Yes Tim.'

Mr Patel stared at the officer but found no words formed in his mouth as the policeman walked with determined steps behind his wife and out of the staffroom. The pharmacist remained still, unsure how to respond. Then, he saw the pack of tampons on the table. He walked quickly out of the staffroom towards the front of the pharmacy. He tried not to notice the long queue of customers waiting for their prescriptions as he hurried to the front door. The couple were about to leave.

'Mrs Baker,' he called out.

The pair turned; Mr Patel saw the policeman was holding his wife's arm in a tight grip.

'You need to come back to the staffroom with me, you've left something in there.'

Natalie stared at the pharmacist then turned away from her husband. Tim Baker loosened his grip of her arm, but started to follow his wife as she walked towards the staffroom. Mr Patel took a breath, then drew himself up to his full five foot three inches of height. He held his right hand up to signal to the police officer to stop.

'I've got this now. You can leave,' he said.

# Control

*By Richard Hooton*

I've known you for so long that I can't imagine life without
you. It's as if you've always been there; a mysterious
presence throughout the mists of time. I can't even
remember when I first knew of your existence. You just
crept into my life until there didn't seem to be a point when
you weren't around, like a plant growing underground
until erupting through to be noticed. Mother, ever the avid
gardener, would compare you to Leylandii, manageable to
begin with before rising to overshadow everything else in
the garden.

You had more patience than anyone in my family. Your
initial appearances were brief and infrequent, just waiting
in the background until emerging ever more familiar. We
became as close as childhood sweethearts and I presumed
we'd be together forever. With that oh-so-useless benefit
of hindsight, Mother tells me now how she could tell when
you were looming, how she could see the changes, how
much anxiety it provoked in her.

'I'd call you "the moods", Sarah,' she said. 'All those
little battles. Stormy one minute, right as rain the next.'

In my teenage years I even thought we were cool, this
romantic, brooding presence: Heathcliff and Cathy on the
moors, Poldark and Demelza in the cornfield. Us against
the world, stomping from dining table to bedroom retreat.
In my head, we were the epitome of leather-clad rebels,
burning with intelligence. With my pale skin, straw-like
hair and crooked nose, I knew I wasn't pretty. Who would
want a fragile, ugly creature like me?

'I'll never leave you.'

That voice, mellow as moonlight, before we disappeared under the duvet for days. As entwined as a married couple, I was gripped. For better, for worse.

It was while trying to find my way in the world that you became difficult. I couldn't get you out of my head. You made me think differently, changed my viewpoint as easily as shifting the face of a Rubik's Cube: a few calculated clicks and I was all blue. You dripped a poisonous cocktail of self-pity, paranoia and angst into my ear. The world was full of charlatans and life was against me. You made me want to be apart from other people.

'Ignore Jane,' you told me. She'd been my best friend since school. 'She looks down on you, mocks you behind your back.' I distanced myself from Jane, screened her calls.

'Don't hang out with Andrew,' you ordered. I'd always got on well with Andrew, since studying together. I really liked him. 'He uses you, frequently cancels, never repays.' I stayed away from Andrew, left his messages unanswered.

'Your mum belittles you.' There was truth wrapped in the lies. Enough to cause doubt that rots into resentment. 'Pull away from her.'

My late teens were aimless, meandering, futile; mostly spent holed up in a bedsit as if we were fugitives.

By my 20syou were an ice age dominating my world. I remember one snowy Christmas, sat in Mother's kitchen looking out at her beloved garden smothered in a white blanket. All life had withered, bleached of colour.

'Everything's dead,' wailed Mother, her harsh grey bob swaying as she viewed the scene with desolate eyes. 'My sunflowers are gone.'

We both burst out in laughter at her melodrama. The release felt like a thawing.

'It'll soon be spring.' She nodded wistfully. 'And then I

can get back out there again.'

Suddenly, without you there, I wanted more, wanted better, wanted to connect. Life isn't staring at bare walls between fighting you off. I'd been contemplating it, in my good moments, I even still had the crumpled college prospectus in my handbag. In a rare flash of decisiveness, I retrieved the brochure and pushed it across the table until it was under her nose.

'There's a hairdressing course I could try.'

She continued to stare at the icicles hanging from her frozen birdbath. 'If that's what you want.'

'It's something I've dreamt of doing.'

She blew on her tea, then sniffed. 'If you think you'll stick at it.'

I vowed there and then to qualify. Practically threw myself at it. I enjoyed learning a new discipline. Loved the softness and pliability of hair between my fingers and influencing its style. Christ, I even liked the responsibility of handling scissors!

But you didn't want me to be free.

I'd grown two lives: with and without you. I needed people to see the upbeat, happier me, not the miserable version when you were there. With you around, people treated me differently; many kept their distance. I'd be flashed a sympathetic yet condescending look that said: "You sure you're all right?" I made excuses for you, pretended the problem was something else. Then, I tried to ignore you.

That was when the real struggle began.

No one likes rejection.

'You'll regret this.' That voice. 'You know what I'm capable of.'

How cancerous becomes a dictator clinging to power?

You chipped away at my confidence, a sculptor hacking

at their creation until nothing's left but dust. Worn out, unable to concentrate, my ambition was exhausted too. My attendance became so poor I had to quit.

I shut myself away again, as if quarantined; didn't want to let you near other people, for them to associate you with me. Embarrassed and ashamed, I hid, like the mad, old woman in the attic, rejecting life.

You had me all to yourself, this anchor chained to my ankle. 'Are you the devil?' I asked, the night I almost succumbed.

I'd thought that I was free of you that evening. Running a bath, I put my hand under the red tap's flow to feel the water's increasing warmth. Once it was full, I settled into the tub, trying to relax.

Then you were there. Pushing me under. A riptide forcing me down.

I held my breath, my only response little bubbles of air that floated to the surface.

A reflex action kicked in. I struggled, pushed back, forced myself up, gasping for oxygen, arms flailing, water splashing over the rim. You'd let go. I clambered out of the bath, dripping all over the floor. I lay there, naked and gulping.

You spoke: 'You don't exist without me.'

I paced the bedsit through the twilight hours, drinking all I had, until the walls converged and I had to get out. Alcohol only numbs pain and fear until its foggy shield dissolves. At dawn, I found Mother on her knees on a small brown mat in her front garden, tending to her sunflowers. She acknowledged my presence with a little wave.

'You all right, dear?'

She squinted in my direction as if looking at a phantom. I didn't have the words. I think I nodded.

'Well you don't look it.'

Neither of us questioned what the other was doing, out and about at first light. We just stared at the sunflowers. Mother competes with herself each year to see how tall she can grow them. She set about spreading fertiliser on the soil around their thick, green stalks as I stood in the street and watched. Then she leant back to admire her handiwork.

Bright, bold and majestic, they were already tall, with manes of golden petals surrounding black heads that reminded me of stereo speakers. Manure overwhelmed any sweet, subtle fragrance.

'They do cheer up the garden,' said Mother. 'And are so easy to look after – as carefree as their smiling faces suggest.'

The sunflowers are positioned by a fence and tethered loosely to stakes with a soft stretch of cloth to protect them from wind and rain. They're covered by netting.

'They're remarkably tough, will grow in any type of soil.' She tells me this every year. Without fail. 'They can tolerate droughts and take a chill or two.' I let out a weary sigh. 'But they still need a lot of attention. And obviously direct sunlight and regular watering.'

Mother climbed to her feet and we looked at the flowers with different expressions on our faces.

'Don't you ever miss Dad?'

She brushed dirt from her gardening gloves. 'There's no point in dwelling on something that happened so long ago.'

Her gaze returned to her creation.

'No matter where you plant them,' she said, 'their faces follow the sunlight and absorb its powerful energy.'

An idea struck me.

She took off the gloves. 'Would you like to come in for a cup of tea, dear?'

I know I shook my head at that. And left without another word.

Hours later, after scraping together what money I could find, I arrived at the airport with a passport and an open mind. I landed in Lanzarote. It was a world away from our grey little island. And you. Neither of us thought I'd have the guts, but I guess it's easier when you're pretending to be someone else.

Stepping off the plane into such sunlight and humidity was like crawling from a cave. At first, I wanted to retreat. But then I began to explore freedom. I listened to waves lapping while browning on the beach.

I read. Ate. Slept.

'How brave,' said the party animals in the neighbouring apartment, when they realized I was holidaying alone.

I drank and danced with them.

Sat at a bar, I swear a cute boy smiled at me.

'Want a drink?' he yelled over the synthesisers. I shook my head, my limit already exceeded.

He leant over, musky aftershave, his lips by my ear. 'How about a dance?'

It was too hot. Uncomfortably close. The air thick. It had to break.

I thought of you.

'Gotta go.'

I left him shrugging his shoulders and stumbled back, the soles of my high heels sticking to my feet.

I hid in my bedroom as lightning flashbulbed the sky and thunder boomed.

Like a developing photograph, you emerged slowly from the shadows. My tears flowed as freely as the rain.

'Why can't you leave me alone?'

I clenched a fist so hard that my false nails drew blood. Threw a glass against a wall. Pounded the bed. I wanted the world to break with me.

'Why me?'

I couldn't sleep with you there. My gloom in the next day's sunshine was as out of place as a pallbearer at a wedding. I cut the break short. You accompanied me on the flight home.

How naïve was I to think you'd just leave me alone? You're never free from such tyranny. You seduced your way back into my consciousness. And like an addict, the temptation to surrender to something so intoxicating is always there. I suppose, despite everything, I couldn't be without you. We'd been together for so long that you were all I knew. Comfort in familiarity. Fear of the unknown.

You took over. My worst enemy my only friend, working insidiously from the inside.

'You're weak, stupid and worthless,' you told me. Any mantra repeated enough will be believed.

I reached my 30s, shipwrecked from society. You can't drift anymore, when you've run aground. Entombed inside my bedsit, benefits swallowed by rent and bills and any savings long wasted, happiness was as far away as the holiday island.

'You'll never be rid of me,' rang through my head.

I had only one option left.

I piled the pills on my bed. Just swallow and it's over. Couldn't do it.

I trudged to a motorway bridge. Headlights sparkled below. I longed to be swept away in their flow. As I looked down I saw Mother standing over my broken body. She was actually crying.

I stepped away.

At the bottom of the darkest pit was a kernel of light. I called her. Then hung up before she answered.

Mother barged her way into my home, trying to mask her disgust at the clutter and dirt: all those unwashed pots and plates, unopened post and piles of clothes.

'Oh, Sarah.' I wasn't used to her eyes locking on mine. To the concern swimming inside them.

'Nothing's wrong,' I said. But everything was.

She grabbed my arms. Held me up as if I were wilting. 'You need help.'

I was too tired to resist.

It was time for a divorce.

She separated us like a boxing referee. Moved me back in with her. Fed me nutritious food. Made sure I drank two litres of water a day. Became a scarecrow watching over me. Insisted I exercised. Took me to a doctor. Ensured I took each pill. Paid for a counsellor. And joined in with the mindfulness sessions.

That kernel grew. She helped untangle it from your ensnaring roots. Made me realise that if I couldn't chop you down, then I'd rise above you to reach the sunshine that you blocked. As my confidence blossomed, I rejoined the human race, running hard to catch up. I returned to my friends and felt able to talk about you, rather than deny.

Sat in a café with Andrew, he told me about the pain of being made redundant and the relief of finding another job. It was then that I realised I'd inherited my father's absence and my mother's disregard.

'I'm so sorry,' I said, crestfallen. 'That I wasn't there for you.'

He smiled. 'Don't worry.' And took my hand. 'It's just good to have you back.' He held it for a little longer than necessary, his skin warm on mine. It felt good.

When Mother deemed me better, she let me return home, though visited me regularly.

In her autumnal garden we surveyed her sunflowers, the tallest a good foot below her previous best. The large browning heads nodded downwards, mildew mottling withered leaves.

'I'll have to remove them,' she said. 'The seeds and stems emit a toxin that inhibits the growth of other plants.'

She looked mournful. I stroked her back, like a groom to an agitated horse.

Her ashen face brightened. 'I'll try again next year.' She turned to me. 'Maybe it's something we can do together?'

I beamed, then faltered. Felt you lurking in the shade, knowing you'll always be there, waiting patiently, ready to emerge when you sense I'm weakening.

Mother pushed a piece of torn newspaper into my hand. 'An ad. For a job. Trainee hairdresser. You could give it a go.'

I looked at the sunflowers. At how tall and strong she'd helped them grow.

'I'd like that.'

I felt lighter. I appreciated then, how I'd learnt how to live with you at my shoulder. And that's enough. Sometimes you're closer, but I'm ready. I know what you're capable of; I survived your worst. And I know you'll never go completely, but I also recognise how far I've come.

You have no form, no substance. You're nothing but a ghost. You may haunt me all my life.

But I have you under control.

# Wilting

*By Maddie Cox*

The petals from the lilies bundled on the kitchen windowsill are beginning to fall; the residual pollen, leaving dull golden stains in their wake. Grace had swiftly removed the decayed leaves, rearranged the bouquet and positioned the fresher flowers in the centre. Standing them tall like regimented soldiers. The bouquet stands proudly, adorning the cheaply grouted kitchen windowsill. Ever the homemaker, she had insisted that they tied the room together, despite their obstruction of sunlight from the garden. The olive-green vase stands between an unlit candle, and an old photo frame. Inside, Grace is enclosed in the arms of a towering man with a slender frame. She glares at the image of the lovers for a while, whilst her tired hands wrap tightly around her china mug, desperate for warmth. The picture was taken about four years prior to their engagement. The younger woman had hair that tumbled beyond her shoulders, her skin was vibrant, and her effervescent grin was boundless. Her upper body was almost hidden entirely by the arms around it. Charlie had always held her like this, constricting her tightly, holding her frame as intently as he could. In the early days, it had made her feel safe. She lets out a strained breath and the corners of her mouth flick upwards slightly. Her train of thought is interrupted by the crash of clumsy footsteps travelling the stairs. Grace smooths down her hair, stands tall and sweeps some residual toast crumbs out of sight.

Charlie bounds through the hallway and hurtles himself towards the sink, taking a newly washed cup from the draining board and hastily filling it with tepid water before chugging the contents, refusing to stop for breath. He wipes his mouth and regains his breath whilst doubled over the sink. Grace wonders whether it is worth bringing her presence to light.

'Morning...' she murmurs apologetically. He turns his bloodshot eyes towards the figure tucked away neatly in the corner. He lets out a strained breath and shunts towards her, snaking his long arms around her waist and shoulders, bringing her tight to his chest, close enough for her to smell the residual cigarette smoke and Jägermeister on his shirt. Before she frees herself from his grasp, he presses his lips into her forehead. She revels in this moment, letting the muscles in her back melt into the limbs surrounding her. Charlie frees the woman from his grasp, and she is reacquainted with the drafty air of the kitchen. Pulling out an old wooden chair from the kitchen table, Charlie sits.

She floats behind him, studying his body from behind. He hadn't had his hair cut for a while, and although she teased him, she secretly liked his freefalling curly mop. She enjoyed pushing it out of his face while he hovered above her on lazy Sundays in bed. She savoured the sweet moments on the sofa where she could twirl the strands between her fingers as they absentmindedly watched TV. As she beams over the mess of chestnut hair before her, her eyes trail down to his neck. She notices something troubling; her eyes meet a small mulberry coloured bruise resting at the nape of his neck, just before his collarbones and partially hidden by his collar. She parts her lips to pose a question, but catches herself before she can make a sound. The lights within her begin to dull as it dawns on her, she has seen that bruise before. It's a mark left in lust, she recognizes it from her heady adolescent days. She feels herself shrink, her body is still in the room but her mind begins to circulate possibilities far beyond. She pictures every eventuality, and every possible reaction before she decides to speak. Mustering all the sweetness she can, Grace chirps,

'Did you have a good night?' He quickly grunts a sound alluding to a '...yeah'. She tightens the grasp on her mug and clears her throat slightly as she replies,

'You got in pretty late...' The air in the room shifts. Charlie straightens his spine, and whips his head turns towards her.

Grace throws him a grin to offset the small pools welling in her eyes. Charlie swiftly flicks his eyes from her hair to her toes and back, assessing her, gauging her body language, shrinking her with his pupils. He continues to look her up and down for a few seconds before turning away from her again, sighing deeply as he readjusts his spine. Grace begins to regret her decision, better to have said nothing. He drums his calloused fingers on the table before muttering,

'...yeah, a few of the boys went back to Joe's, had some beers...' Grace replies,

'Oh... sounds nice.' She turns away from Charlie and towards the sink. He was lying, and Grace knew him enough to know the cadence of his voice when he was guilty. She had been here enough times to know what the tautness in the air often culminated in. Wanting to maintain neutrality, Grace began to wipe down the kitchen surfaces while she internally analyzed her next move. Charlie had never responded well to feeling cornered. Like a frightened stray, upon any sense of a trap, his reactions are often unpredictable. Whenever Grace raised an issue, she learned to coat her words in layers of sweetness and subtlety. This had become a default tactic. Not just in conversations with Charlie, but throughout her life. She always hopes to blend into the wallpaper of whatever room she finds herself in.

Never wanting to be noticed, or scrutinized. She makes herself malleable to whichever hands hold her. She poises herself, and rehearses her next sentence in her head, before tossing it into the room as if it isn't a live grenade.

'So, Joe is back from his week away then...right?'

'How did you know that?' Charlie barks instinctively. His eyes deepen as he realizes he has incriminated himself. He stands and starts to pace the room. Grace pretends not to notice his rising temper and replies.

'I saw Louise's...' Before Grace can finish the sentence, Charlie turns his frame toward her and territorially maneuvers towards her corner of the kitchen. He stops, just before he reaches the corner of tiles she had confined herself to.

'Louise?' He spits out her name as if it is an unpleasant taste to him. Grace had not had time to deconstruct her response, she scolds herself silently, she knows better. She doesn't respond, she needs more time.

'You said you deleted her from your phone.' Charlie smirks as he knows he has given himself the high ground, and he uses his vantagepoint to pounce.

'I did... well, I just checked in on her. She's not as bad as you think, y'know, she just wanted to know...' Any calming measures Grace had put in place had now been decimated.

Charlie turns his back to her and paces to the other side of the kitchen, throwing his spindly arms in the air in an obnoxious display of disbelief.

'You were messaging her?' He sprays a glare of disgust across the room, showering her in his disdain. 'You remember what you were like when you were friends with her? Before we met? You were a mess.'

Charlie was referring to Grace's University days. Her, Louise, and a few other mutual friends of theirs, made a habit of going on Friday night drinking sprees. Grace would wear the most scandalous outfit in her closet, drink far too much and dance as if her limbs were not attached to her body. She would often take it too far, and find herself with a sore head, and some embarrassing stories that she would rather have forgotten. But it was a time of excess and exploration. It was at this time that Grace and Charlie had met. Louise brought her boyfriend Joe and his statuesque hometown friend, Charlie. As soon as he saw her, he made conquering Grace's affections his mission. Grace remembered that he was incredibly self-assured, he talked to her as if he already knew her, and at times she believed he did.

This is what had drawn Grace to Charlie in the first place. He strode into her life, boasting a shadow to hide within. Grace learned to love the dark places she retreated to within the shade he cast. Whenever she pulled away from him, she felt exposed. The cruel and unflattering parts of herself were out in broad daylight. Within him she could hide herself from scrutiny.

The chill travelling through her spine brings Grace back to the present. The shame wraps itself around her stomach. She breathes shakily and replies,

'Yeah...yeah I know. I'm sorry.' She begins to shuffle her feet toward Charlie's end of the kitchen; his sharp inhale lets her know that she is not welcome.

'So, where were you?' Grace asks as an uncharacteristic sense of defiance fills her. Charlie's spine stiffens even further, and his shoulders draw back.

'Does it matter? Don't you trust me?' Grace did not have a definitive answer to either question. She remained silent. She hopes in this moment that he will remember that he loves her. Grace hopes that maybe, within the quiet, he will turn his gaze into a tender and comforting apology, rather than the vicious and pointed glare that is burning through her skin. He looks at her with a smug disdain, the way Hannibal looks at Clarice. Every second his gaze covers her, she feels all her flaws bubbling to the surface. Every mistake, every misstep, everything she hated about herself is laid out bare on the kitchen tiles, like toys for Charlie to play with. And as he stands there, deciding which will give him the most satisfaction, she is totally at his mercy.

'We were at Mollie's.' He let these words fall and delights in watching her fail to catch her breath. The corners of his mouth dart upwards for a split second as he revels in the power he has. Charlie knows the weight his words hold, and knowing that he has the power to make Grace cry gives him a twisted reassurance of her love.

'Your ex?' she asks, not wishing to hear an answer. Charlie nods, proudly.

'And no, before you ask, I didn't fuck her. Maybe I should have though, you're here throwing out all these accusations.' Charlie observes Grace as she lets the tears she had been desperately choking back, fall. She thinks that maybe if he sees that she is weak, he might relent.

The pangs of guilt within Charlie's stomach further fuel his anger, he doesn't allow her to have the power to make him feel guilty. He bounds towards her until his toes cross the corner-tiles she is tucked within. As he stands over her, he feels powerful as he notes how small she seems in comparison. Through almost gritted teeth, he spits out the words that hurt her most,

'You act fucking mental sometimes, you know that? Always on my back, accusing me of something. It's like you don't give a shit about me.'

Grace is blubbering like a child. Her nose is running, and her breath escapes her. She raises her hands to hold

Charlie's head, to try to make him see her, to bring some comfort to them both. In a desperate plea she wails.

'Babe... pl—'

Before she can reach him, he turns, and snatches the olive vase within his long fingers. Grace freezes in shock. He stands above her, with the vase over his head, his nostrils flaring. He draws his arm back further as he launches the vase from his clutch. Grace squeezes her eyes shut and brings her forearms in front of her face trying to make herself as small as she can. The sound of an ear-splitting shatter fills the room. The birds in the garden trees flee. As the noise escapes the room, Grace slowly peeks her head above her forearms, she sees the shattered green clay at her feet. The dead flowers are sprawled across the fresh, blanketed within shards. Charlie is panting. The couple both look at each other in utter disbelief. Charlie turns and grabs his coat; he takes the keys to their car and slides through the backdoor without saying another word.

When Grace hears the car's tires disturb the stones of the driveway, she knows he is gone. She breathes a desperate sigh and falls with her back to the kitchen counter. She reaches her hands to the counter behind her to steady herself. The cool granite alerts her to how clammy her hands have become. As she takes a moment to assess her surroundings, her breath slows to a neutral pace. The fragments of clay surround her bare feet. She reaches to the cabinet above her to remove a dustpan and brush. As she sweeps the remnants, a piece tumbles from the bristles. Grace attempts to pick it up with her fingers, in doing so, the fragment leaves a slight yet deep cut in her index finger. She brings the wound to her mouth as if sucking the poison from a snake bite.

The sun is now disappearing from the bottom of the garden. As Grace stands watching the light fade, she sips a cooled glass of Chenin-Blanc (a bottle she had been saving for tonight's dinner). The wine is nearing its end and the meal she had prepared has been relegated to the freezer. In the absence of the vase, she notices the golden hue from the sunset illuminating the tiles in a way that she hadn't seen before. As Grace surveys the kitchen, she notes the silence that fills their home. Charlie's presence was always so distinct, his noise was more comforting than the deafening quiet he leaves in his wake. His thunder could encompass Grace's own inner storms. Her eyes once again wander to the image of the two young sweethearts. Envy fills her, she thinks back to the life of the woman in the photograph, how she was unrestrained. She dwells for a moment on the many futures that this woman could have had and wonders how she ended up with this one. The lives she was capable of float in front of her for a moment and taunt her, she pushes them sharply out of her mind, not wishing to grieve them anymore.

Grace had taken the remnants of the Chilean wine up to bed with her and nursed the last drops whilst slipping into her pyjamas. An old T-shirt of Charlie's, splattered in the remnants of the paint they had used to redecorate the living room. As her head succumbs to the pillow, she is alerted to movement by the sound of the stones on the driveway. The front-door opens shyly as solemn footsteps follow. The plodding steps of heavy boots grow until they reach the bedroom door. Three slow knocks proceed.

'Come in...' Grace's tired voice bleats.

The threshold is suddenly filled by an imposing frame. From the moonlight coming through the hallway window, Grace can make out that Charlie is cradling something in his arms. She rolls to her side slightly and flicks the bedside lamp on. Grace can see her husband, eyes sullen, hair wet, clutching a vase of flowers.

# Agape

## By Abbie Lewis

This karaoke night was unlike any other. Every
Thursday, the hotel staff went to Jim's bar to perform the
same replication of the song, 'Summer Nights' from the 70s
movie classic '*Grease*.' But, there was something in the air
that night.

'Mila, come on we sing this every week. You're the
Danny to my Sandy,' Louisa nagged, trying to pull her onto
the stage, 'Oh I see, you fancy that guy over there.'
    He was the best dressed, and best-looking guy Mila had
seen all season. His large nose, straight from the base to
the tip, complemented his chiseled jawline. His dark brown
hair, long eyelashes and olive skin suggested he was a
Greek local. When she caught hold of his big brown eyes,
she got a fluttery feeling in her stomach.
    'Go on, go get his number then,' Louisa giggled.
    'Grow up, Louisa. What are the lyrics again?' She was
never really the type to approach anyone. Her whole life
she was told she wasn't good enough and no one would
ever love her. Usually, you would ignore these comments,
but when your mother drills them into you, it's almost
impossible. Most boys were drawn to her. She was one of
those Polly Pocket kind of girls. Innocent looking with big
blue eyes and long blonde hair other girls would die for.
    Mila had been working in Mykonos for five months
now, and her fondness for the country grew each day. She
fell in love with the island because of the people. Their
friendliness and open-arm attitudes were different from
what she had experienced growing up. Her home life

was miserable, she grew up in a council estate in Boston where the noise was harrowing, and her mother was a dysfunctional alcoholic. It would be a miracle if she came home from work and there weren't empty beer bottles clogging up the table, and her mother wasn't screaming at some rubbish on the TV. The anger would then often transfer to her.

'You're useless.'

'Council estate scum.'

'No one will ever love you!'

'Look at your fucking ugly hair.'

'What are you wearing?'

She threw all kinds of abuse at her. When Mila saw the Twitter advertisement for hotel activity instructors in Mykonos, and that they required no qualifications, it wasn't a question for her. Two weeks later, she was stepping off the plane to the beaming sunshine hitting her skin.

She'd made a conscious effort to learn generic greetings, "*kalimera*" (good morning) and "*kalispera*" (good evening) and the locals welcomed her openly for her sweet nature and warm smile. She loved the tranquility of the island. Despite the lively atmosphere the strip gave off, the buzz faded as she entered the quiet street of her apartment. But Thursday night was karaoke night, and she knew she could not let Louisa down by not participating in their weekly duet.

She was just about to crack out the 'oh well oh well oh well oh, uh' when she noticed in the corner of her eye that he was paying his bill.

*It's now or never*, she thought.

As she felt the burn on her tongue and throat from taking a confidence shot of tequila, she turned around, and he had appeared at her table.

'Layland,' he took out his hand, 'I couldn't leave and

not introduce myself. You're really beautiful.' His use of accented vowels confirmed his Greek status, which added to his charm.

'Hi, I'm Mila.' At this point, the fluttery feeling in her stomach had exploded; she felt warmth around him she never knew possible.

That rest of the night was a blur. She looked at her second-hand Michael Kors watch and noticed it had been five hours since the introduction and yet it felt like minutes. They had been talking and drinking, discovering each other's childhoods and what had brought them to that same bar that night. Not just because they fancied a drink but the meaningful butterfly effect that got them there, at this moment she felt his name was fitting, it means protector of man, and when she was with him, she did feel protected.

The following two months, she longed for the working day to be over because it meant she got to see him. She'd got to know his family and began to see them as her own. Her mother had taught her how to cook traditional dishes like moussaka and dolmades. Her sister had taken her shopping and transformed her wardrobe, from black leather and lace to striped relaxed dresses, blue denim jackets and dungarees. He was caring and complimentary, but also the life and soul of the party, and he showed her off like she was his queen. For the first time, she felt truly happy and excited about the future. She felt like she had come out the end of a dark tunnel, and finally, the sun shone brightly down on her. Was it too soon to believe she loved him?

On an Autumn morning, they had decided to go for a walk along the beach before she started work. Darkness had not long given way to the light, and the sky appeared diffused with peach and magenta. The waves in the majestic blue ocean tapped their feet as they strolled along the shore. Her hair was being sent into different directions with the warm breeze swirls.

'Baby, what do you think of getting a new job? One that pays better?'

She hesitated for a second as she loved her job.

'If you earned more money, we could get our place and start a family. Imagine a mini us running around the garden. You would love that.'

He saw a future with her, and this thrilled her so much, for a minute, her rational senses had gone out the window.

'I guess I could have a look.'

'I've got you an interview tonight. We can get our apartment in no time.'

As they entered the bar, a slender older man greeted them. He narrowed his eyes and examined her closely. Looking her up and down then saying something to Layland in Greek before handing him a wad of euros.

'So, you're happy to do this job?' He directed the question to Mila, but before she could answer Layland had replied,

'Yes, she's fine.'

He squeezed her hand, which reassured her there was nothing to worry about. Looking back, Mila wondered would her life be different if she ever questioned what 'job' meant.

From the bar, Layland took her straight to a lavish-looking hotel. Tall with infinity pools to every room.

'We can't afford this?' she looks at him, open-eyed and confused.

'Just take this up to room seventeen A, he'll instruct you from there,' he shoved an envelope into her hand, and she goes without question.

A short, plump man opened the door and instructed her to come in. As he went and locked the door behind her, she had a sudden rush of fear. She assessed the room. A single bed caged into a small space. The curtains were shut, and there was a ring-light beside a video camera on a tripod. She tried to escape, but he grabbed her and shoved her down onto the bed. He took off his belt and struck her with it before he flipped her onto her back, pulled up her dress and ripped her pants off. She wanted to cry and scream, but every muscle in her body had frozen. This man's soul had died. The pain was excruciating when he forced himself inside her. Every time she closed her eyes- it felt like it was happening again. She felt him forcing his way into her; she smelt his body odour and bad breath.

Then it was over, and he pushed her out the door, shoving money into her hand. It was like nothing had happened and she must pretend everything is okay.

She stumbled down the hotel stairs, out the lobby and threw herself in his arms. Every emotion hit her, and she stood sobbing like a child weeping to its mother.

'What's wrong, you're shaking,' he squeezed her tight.

'I can't do this job. We can find another way to make money.'

'There is no other way. It won't be for long. Soon we'll have enough money that we will never have to work again,' he said, 'Now pass it to me, I'll save it for us.'

Without question, she handed it to him and knew there had to be a justified reason for doing this because he loves her.

She got home and hurried to the shower. When the water ran down her, she tried to wash away the smell and sweat of the man who raped her and yet no amount of soap took it away.

After that day, she worked as an escort. Most days she would do six to twelve jobs, each lasting between a few minutes to an hour. Layland would tell her who to sleep with, he took control of her finances and her self-esteem grew smaller every day. He made her believe he loved her and everything he got her do was for their future. At the same time, he distanced her from her old friends under the guise they did not have her best interest. She became dependent on him for everything.

There was a regular client who was into whips and chains. He often tied her to the bed and the sex would last for hours. When she cried out, begging him to stop, it gave him a kick and he would tighten the handcuffs.

'I'm not hurting you.' But it did hurt.

She became severely underweight and couldn't imagine being at all attractive; but these men didn't care what she looked like; they were so desperate for sex they were in control of it. Most clients would want quick sex, some even just wanted company, and some would want unimaginable things. Some would even insist on urinating on her face. A lot of them used condoms, but the occasional person didn't, they paid more. Mila thought they were always the dirtiest, but Layland would reassure her they had health checks, and they were never allowed to finish inside her.

But one day, Layland was dropping her off to a hotel room and warned her,

'Don't fuck this one up. He's paying a lot.

When she arrived, he offered her a large vodka and orange.

*Don't fuck this one up.*

She accepted the drink politely. Hours later she woke up lying next to the rapist in bed. She knew he must had laced the alcohol with drugs. She remembered sitting on the bed, talking to him about his work as a banker, and she had a faint recollection of him tentatively cupping her breast. But she couldn't remember anything else. She fumbled for her clothes and silently crept towards the door as her feet wobbled. She had the tell-tell stickiness between her legs. She felt like someone had punched her in the stomach, and in that second, she finally began to hate Layland.

When he was waiting for her outside the hotel, she shouted abuse at him. She no longer cared if this would upset him or if he would react in anger. Everything came out.

'Get away from me, you fucking monster!' Tears sprang into her eyes because she had finally seen him for who he was. At this moment, she could see through the false sense of love and protection, and her need to be cared for and realised he had been playing a wicked game with her.

He looked at her wide-eyed and astonished.

'You ungrateful little slag!' he twisted his fingers in her hair and yanked her into the car, hitting her head on the door on the way in, 'Are you done making a scene? We have to work hard now to enjoy our future.

*We*, she thinks, *there is no we*. He was not being degraded and humiliated day in and out. *How dare he*.

'I'm so sorry. Baby, please forgive me. I want the best for us, and sometimes I get angry when I think it's not going to happen. I promise it won't happen again.' He was trying to kiss her, but she turned her face away.

She wondered why she'd never noticed the darkness in his eyes before and how she could have trusted him so implicitly for so long. His face right now was as cold as a winter's day; his brown eyes were black now. His chiseled cheekbones now resembled that of a monster, and she no longer saw the charm in his domineering persona.

Days passed, and he began to monitor her a lot more. He dropped her to jobs and was there when she finished. The doors were locked when they got home, and she was only allowed to get fresh air under his watch. He had threatened her family and told her if she went to the police, she would be in trouble for prostitution. It would be easy to dissolve into a panic now, to let her body show the terror and helplessness she felt, but this wasn't going to help her escape. It wasn't until Mila had been sent to a hotel where she was expected to sleep with a wealthy, filthy politician that it clicked. It was rare that Layland wouldn't be waiting outside the front. But this is a hotel, of course, there's a back exit. She glanced up at the fire exit sign, *It's now or never.*

Slowly, she pushed through the door, taking care not to let anyone see her and peeped around the corner. There it was at, the end of the road. The beach they had gone to the day Layland asked her to get a new job.

She felt the cold splashes on her bruise covered skin. They say drowning is a relaxing way to die. One minute your head is bobbing above the water, and then the pain is gone. She wasn't afraid anymore. As she began to fall further into the darkness, for the first time in months, she finally felt clean.

# Lost

## *By Jen Hall*

'Excuse me, you dropped something.' I call at a man.
It doesn't look important, this thing. It fell out his back
pocket; it could be a receipt. But it might be a train ticket.
Or a locker receipt – you can leave bags and coats on
hangers in museums nowadays.

He doesn't turn around at the sound of my voice, but it's
a busy street. How would he know it's him I'm talking to?
I walk over and pick it up. It is a train ticket. For a morning
train, with a stamp on it to say it's been used. The stamp is
a raised impression and in slightly green ink. It's probably
rubbish. He may not notice he's lost it. Or he might need it.
People need receipts for expenses; you have to prove that
you bought things to prove you're not stealing. I get my
trolley and follow after him.

He's walking briskly; he has somewhere to go. It's a
struggle to keep up. I'm slower than him as I have all my
things. The bottom of my trolley sags and drags along the
pavement sometimes, and the wheels splay out. But it's
still useful. Easier than carrying all my bags. The bags are
important to keep things organised.

Finally, the man turns into a quieter road, and I'm
relieved I've caught up with him. He hears me this time
when I shout: 'Excuse me sir, you dropped this.'

He looks at me, and barely glances at the ticket I'm
holding out towards him.

'It's not mine.' he says. He has that dismissive voice,
and a frown on his face. As if I can't possibly have
anything of his. It reminds me of my husband when I told
him I was pregnant.

*It's not mine.*

'It is. I saw you drop it.' *It is, it can't be anyone else's.*

'It doesn't matter anyway.' *You can't prove it's mine.* He walks away. I tuck the ticket into a bag in my trolley. I have a bag for paperwork. Receipts, bills, letters. A lot of train tickets. It's important to keep hold of things. You never know when you might start to miss them. If I have things organised, I might be able to help when someone realises what they've lost. I turn my trolley and walk back the way I came, back towards my part of town.

It's a loud night tonight. It must be a weekend. Boys shouting. Girls shrieking – in fun most of the time. I don't think I hear any pain. It's dark, but the heat of the day is still here. The air smells of warm tarmac. The ground is dry. People lose different things at this time of year. They don't have all the extras needed for winter – no gloves or scarves or extra coats. In this weather, people lose sunglasses. Or beads dropping from broken necklaces. Sometimes girls lose shoes in this weather. High-heeled, strappy ones. They can walk barefoot on the streets when they're dry and warm. It's dangerous – you might step in dog mess, cigarette butts or glass. But falling off those shoes looks dangerous too. I feel proud of these girls with the confidence to walk and throw caution to the wind. They hardly even need their shoes.

*I bring you everything you need.* The words drummed into my head are still there now.

I keep hold of their shoes. Just in case. Maybe in the daylight their confidence would drop away, and they'd need their shoes.

A boy drops some food. I don't like talking to boys; it can be dangerous. But he might be hungry later. I hesitate for a moment while I decide, then the words burst out of me.

'You dropped something!' I shout at him. He hears me and looks towards me. I point at his food, and he replies to me.

'Why don't you pick it up then? Lazy cow!' His friends laugh.

I blink at his words, and the echo they create from another time. *It's a tip in here. What do you do all day? Lazy cow.*

It's safer not to argue. I drop my pointed finger, and curl my arm back in. The boy is walking towards me.

'I said you should pick it up,' he says, standing in front of me. I don't want to leave my things. I'm worried about my things. But it's easier to do what they ask. Less chance of violence. Perhaps.

*Do some fucking cleaning for once.*

I walk over to his food and pick it up.

'Now put it in the bin. You don't deserve my leftovers.'

*You don't deserve to eat. I have to work. You can have some food when you've worked for it.*

I close the polystyrene lid and drop it carefully into the bin. He walks away. I could feel that it was still hot. I wait until he's definitely gone before I collect it from the bin.

A woman drops a pound coin at my feet.

'You dropped this!' I say and hold it out to her. I start to get up, to follow her and return it.

'It's for you, don't get up.' My legs start to ache as I crouch between sitting and standing. I'm not sure what to do now.

*You sit on your arse all day. Get out of my way you stupid bitch.* There's never a right answer.

'Do you need a hot drink?' she asks. I shake my head. Hot drinks can be dangerous.

*Stupid Cow! You've burnt my tongue.* A long-gone scream rattles around my head as too-hot coffee is poured over my baby. *See – you'd have made me drink something that hot?* Best to stay away from hot drinks.

'Anything to eat? I could get you a sandwich?' The woman is still there, looking at me. I can feel tears boiling up in my head. I didn't think I could cry any more.

A different voice repeats in my head this time. A neighbour, shouting through my letter box. *You're worse than an animal. Letting him starve like that.*

This woman in front of me is talking to me like I'm a person. I carry on getting up, gathering my things. Time to move on. She's seen me, but I can't let her see the real me. I feel her disappointment in me as I move down the street.

I'm trying to read my book in the park. My eyes are still good, but the light is too bright. The book was lost. I found it near a bench, but I didn't see anyone drop it. I sat on the bench and held it for a while in case someone came back. Sometimes people don't realise when they've lost something.

I waited with the book for a whole day. I hear a policeman's voice, an echo of disgust from years ago. *You just sat there and waited while he died.*

Lots of people walk one way to work, and then the same way back again. Someone might have come past looking for it. I put it on the bench beside me. I don't mean to, but I think I make things invisible.

*Why didn't you try and get help?*

People try so hard not to see me, that they don't see the things around me either.

I sit quietly, and hope I'm doing the right thing. If I'm just waiting, nothing bad that happens is my fault.

*Why didn't you try and get help?*

I tried to help that person who lost their book. The book is mine now. I waited long enough.

A baby drops a sock off the end of its toes. That happens

a lot. Baby socks are one of the things I have most of. That and gloves. Odd gloves, one at a time. Rarely a pair. Enough for a bag full. Sometimes I give the gloves to my friends when it is really cold. The ones I've had the longest, that people are definitely not coming back for.

'Your baby dropped a sock,' I call, and the woman looks back. She sees it lying, lost on the pavement.

'Thank you,' she says to me. She puts the sock back on to her kicking baby. Mumbling about what a pickle he is. She saw me. She heard me. Voices from people I've never even met jumble in my head. Voices on television, people in the supermarket, jumping out from the newspaper.

*Didn't anyone hear the baby crying?*

The sock wasn't lost.

*Social Services should have been checking on them.*

If people notice me, I can make sure things aren't lost.

# Monster Circus

*By E.S. Welsh*

The trees hunched their backs against the wind, long arms grasping for company in the gale. The forest stretched on endlessly, bending down to close Michael in. He couldn't focus as his stomach yowled in protest, still begging for some sort of sustenance. He wanted to fall into the dirt and scream for help until his voice gave out.

'But they'll find you…' A small voice in the back of his head whispered to him. Branches scratched his bare flesh as he pushed his way through the dense foliage, trying to stay off the forest path. 'They'll find you.' The voice whispered again as he stumbled over a thick tree root that poked out of the uneven ground.  A gust of wind blew suddenly through the leaves, pushing its way through Michael's frail body.

His clothes offered no protection from the cold, the shirt was made out of a loose, thin, white fabric that Michael didn't know the name of. It was filled with newly made holes. His trousers were navy and stopped just above his ankle; the fabric was ripped and frayed, stained with mud. The brown shoes he wore were caked in mud as well; the shoes themselves were a size too small and crushed his toes with each step.

Michael leant against an oak tree to regain his breath; he must have been walking for hours. Rubbing a hand over his screaming stomach in a vain attempt to sooth it. Michael glanced around. The silence of the forest broke when the sound of a whistle echoed through the trees.  'I must be hallucinating,' he thought, drinking in the stillness of his surroundings.  'A whistle in the forest, why would there be a whistle in a forest?' He mused. He almost laughed; he would have, if it didn't hurt to do so.

The whistle blew again, this time it was louder, more high-pitched than the whistles he had heard on the prison yard. Michael pushed himself off the tree whipping his head around in every direction. 'What in God's name?' Michael uttered, momentarily forgetting his hunger. His legs burned and his stomach felt as if it had begun to eat itself. He pushed his body onwards, occasionally resting on a tree to catch his breath or to sooth his aching limbs.

Michael felt his eyes droop, as the commands of his body took over. The pain became too much to bear, he wanted to collapse, to disappear into a bush and let the ground swallow him whole, anything to have some peace. He slumped down the bark of a pine, the back of his shirt raised as he fell – the bark ran its wooden fingers down his back. His breathing slowed and small tears fell down his bruised cheeks.

*I'm done…* He thought.

The whistle pierced through the silence forcing his eyes open. Plumes of white smoke cut through the green of the leaves like a shining sword, squinting, Michael watched the smoke come closer and closer. A chugging sound then a screech of metal wheels sliding to a halt stabbed away the silence and made Michael's heart leap up into his throat.

'That sounds like…' Michael began as he pushed himself to stand, the moss on the trunk moist under his spindly fingers.

Thin wooden tracks were embedded in the bottom of the ravine, leaves and roots had grown over the tracks twisting them out of place. It looked as if it would break if someone stood on it let alone hold a steam engine.

The train rolled smoothly on the rails, twelve compartments long, large rectangle crates stacked on top of small metal wheels. Each compartment was brightly coloured, hand painted designs of exotic animals and people in vibrant costumes labelled each side. Michael smiled. 'Run away and join the circus, huh?' He mumbled to himself, 'Never thought it would happen.' Mustering up as strength he could, he made his way down the ravine, slipping and sliding down the muddy slope.

*

The door to the eighth compartment was painted gold and silver with the letters M and B in flowing script, Michael pushed on it. It creaked open making him wince.

Inside was grand, like something out of a palace. Long pieces of fabric hung across the ceiling, different shades of red and purples, falling over the windows. Sunlight streamed in through the gaps, splashing the room with magenta hues. A small circular table with several bottles of multi-coloured liquids sat in the middle of the carriage. In the corner was a wooden desk with piles of papers spread across it. On the far wall were posters of the circus, ageing and frayed, of the acts. Michael stepped in further, he noticed a white dressing table with clothes flung all over it. Bottles tipped over, staining the white with creams and blues. 'What a mess!' He thought, glancing round to see any inhabitants.

He stepped over a pile of foul smelling clothes, pushing on a wooden screen for balance. The screen wobbled. He tried to catch it before it fell, but it was too late. It fell crushing against a narrow bed and there was a loud scream. Michael jumped back, falling down, hitting his head on the edge of the dressing table. 'Who are ya?' A shrill voice screamed. 'How did ya get on this train?'

Michael rubbed the back of his head, his vision blurred slightly. Bottles wobbled and fell on the carpeted floor, spilling their contents. Through the blurriness he could make out the shape of a woman clutching a large piece of cloth over her chest.

'I said, who are ya?' She demanded, tugging the blanket closer to her chest.

Michael's vision cleared and he saw her, dressed only in a blanket. Smeared makeup covered her entire face; there were black rings around her grey eyes. Cherry red stained her lips and some of her cheek. Her chin was pointed and freckles peppered the bridge of her nose and neck. Thick golden hair stuck up in every direction. She was beautiful, yet Michael could tell that she was dangerous. It was something with the way her features were drawn, an angelic frame hiding a deadly secret. Michael felt his heart sink; he had thought he stumbled into the storage carriage, but there she was standing over him, one hand clutching the blanket the other reaching for something behind her.

Michael opened his mouth to apologise, to beg, to say something that would allow him to stay, but nothing came out. He just laid there with his mouth agape.

She frowned at him, 'Are you deaf or somethin'?' Michael shook his head quickly.

'Well, answer me damn question,'

'I'm…I'm… Lewis.' Michael lied. The woman nodded, relaxing slightly, a little too quickly for Michael's liking.

'I'm Madame Bath, I own this mad house.' She gestured to her surroundings, she became oddly calm, a man had broken into her carriage after all, he expected her to run into the next carriage screaming, but she just stood there watching him. Michael followed her movements; she seemed to make the dimly lit room shine. Madame Bath smiled, wrapping the blanket around her chest and securing it tightly by tucking the corner into the edge.

'So what brings ya to my train, Lewis?' She purred his fake name, as she sat by her desk.

Michael slowly stood, blinking franticly to get rid of

the blurriness. He could hear her laugh in the far corner of the carriage. 'Ya an odd one, ya know, Lewis.' She said, twirling around in her chair.

'Erm…don't you want to get dressed?' Michael asked looking everywhere but her bare legs. Madame Bath shrugged and fiddled with her hair; she turned to him fully and smirked.

'What are ya doing on me train, Mister Lewis?' She asked again, Michael gulped. Just lie, it's easy, you've been doing it all your life. He opened his mouth again, as before words seemed to fail him. Glancing around, he tried to focus on something, to create a believable lie to allow him to stay. His eyes rested on the poster of an acrobat – no that wouldn't work, he could bare the sequined leotard if it meant he could keep his freedom, the height however that was another story. The next was a strongman; he wasn't anything impressive when it came to strength. Each poster held a quality he wanted, strength, flexibility, bravery.

'I…I want a job.' He blurted out.

Madame Bath raised an eyebrow at this outburst, but she smiled sweetly at him. 'Well, then Mister Lewis. We are gonna need ya to audition. You'll have until the next stop to prepare something for us either that or…' She paused, her smile disappeared. 'Or, we call the police and send ya back to whatever sewer they put ya in.'

Michael's heart sank further, did she know? Wait, how did she know? Madame smiled, 'I know everything, darlin," She purred answering his unspoken question, her hand resting on a newspaper. The headline read: **Man escapes prison. The manhunt begins.** Beneath was a picture of him, dressed in his uniform. He looked clean shaven in the photo and there was no possible way to tell his hair was red from the grainy black and white photo. Michael glanced away from the paper and into Madame

Bath's eyes.

'So, do we have a deal?' She asked softly.

# A Quiet Drink

## By Les Clarke

The man looked around the bar, checking everyone out.
I like being by myself. It suits my personality. I like the
quiet. I don't like crowds, unless I'm working and then
sometimes they can be beneficial to me. I can hide amongst
'em. Generally, I like to keep myself to myself, ya know. I
enjoy my own company. I don't get lonely. I've always got
too much going on. Ya see most of the time my job ain't
easy, so I like to kinda look back and reflect on how it's
all starting to pan out and take shape. My job ain't straight
forward. Generally, I gotta do a lot of background research
and stuff like that to make it work. No loose ends. Never. I
can't allow that. And, in a job like mine, that can involve a
certain amount of risk.  He allowed himself a small smile.
But hey, that's part of the attraction I guess. So as I say, I
like to drink alone, and be left alone.  People should respect
that. That ain't a lot to ask. But ya know what some people
are like. They just 'won't listen to reason.'
   So, there I was, I'd been up near Grand Central Station,
doing some research, and all I wanted was a nice cold
drink, and the chance to just reflect on a few things. I
was sitting in this bar when I saw this guy move up to the
counter a few seats away, and he started looking at me. I
don't mean a passing glance or something like that, I mean
he was looking at me like he had me under a goddamn
microscope or something. I could feel his eyes boring right
into me, and I don't take too kindly to that kinda intrusion,
especially when I was just trying to chill out, ya know.  I
turned and looked at the guy, and he looked right back
at me, and gave me a single nod of the head, as if he had

acknowledged he knew me or something. Well, I ain't never set eyes on him before, I never forget a face. It don't pay to forget faces in my line of work. He just carried on looking right back at me. This went on for a short time, and then this guy came up to the stool beside me and said,

'Is anybody sitting there?'

I didn't turn round, I just said, 'Yeah, the invisible man!' And he laughed at that, and just sat himself right down beside me as if that was an actual invite to do so. Then he stuck out his hand and said,

'Hi, I'm Andy.'

'And that involves me how?' I said. This guy was starting to bug me. All I wanted was a quiet drink. What I did not want, was for some sales person or goddamn faggot to start hitting on me. Unless this guy had a liking for hospital food, he needed to get his ass as far away from me as he could in double quick time. But no, oh no, he started trying to engage me in conversation. So, I turned towards this guy, and held his gaze. I locked eyes with this guy, so he'd have no trouble understanding what I was about to say to him, and then I said,

'I don't talk to strangers.' And d'ya know what this guy said to me? I mean, you ain't gonna believe what this guy said to me.

He said, 'A stranger is a friend you just haven't met yet.' And then he smiled this sickly smile at me, and right there and then, I tell ya, I felt like busting him right in the middle of his sanctimonious smile. Whoever the hell this guy was, he wasn't easily fazed, I'll give him credit for that. He then asked me if I wanted a drink. I didn't bother answering, but he went right ahead and ordered me another J.D. and just slid it across in front of me. Well, if he was waiting for me to thank him, he was in for a l-o-n-g wait. I didn't ask for the drink, so following that line o' reason, I wasn't about to thank him for it either. He then asked if I was waiting for someone. I suppose I coulda said, yeah, and maybe then he woulda backed off and gone and started talking to someone else. But I kept silent, and he stayed put.

After his remark about strangers being friends and all, I figured him for some kinda religious nut, and religion is w-a-y down the list of things that play a part in my life. So I kept schtum. But I dunno, I think this guy mistook silence for some kinda challenge, and he started up again. Giving me his opinions on what was wrong with the world, and how things could be changed, blah-de-blah-de-blah. Oh boy, this guy was really starting to get to me, and in the end I just said to him,

'Whatever it is you're sellin' I ain't buying!'

And he says to me, he says, 'Buddy, all I'm doing is making conversation.'

And I said, 'No! What you're doing is making me angry, 'cos all I want is to be left alone to finish my goddamn drink, conversation is the last thing I'm looking for!'

But he stayed put. He just sat there moving his glass around between his hands, like he was making something outa clay, ya know, moulding it into some kinda shape. And after a few moments he turned to me and he said,

'Why are you so angry with me?'

I mean the nerve of this guy, can you believe that?

I said, 'I'm angry because you ain't listenin' to what I'm saying! I don't want your conversation, I don't want your drink, and I definitely don't want your company! What I want, is for you to just butt out and leave me alone. That's what I want!'

So, he looked up at me with this sad-eyed puppy dog kinda hurt look and says, 'I didn't mean nothing by it. Look I play this game ya know, where I look at a person and then try to work out what it is they do. Ya know for work.

It kinda passes the time. I had ya down for a construction worker but then I figured no that ain't it. And then I thought maybe ya was in some kinda corporate job, but that didn't seem to fit either …'

I cut him off. 'What the hell does it matter,' I said. 'I just wanted to finish my drink and go home. So I said, 'It's none of your business what I do. So just leave me alone, Kapish?'

'Aw just tell me' he says, 'it ain't such a big deal. Tell me and then I'll go. No one's ever been like this to me before; everyone else has always told me.'

So I made the decision to tell him, if for no other reason, than to just get rid of him. So I told him straight, I said … 'I kill people.' Hah! His face was a goddamned picture! I swear to God his jaw hit the counter! He just stood there open-mouthed. That bought me a quiet moment or two I can tell ya.

So then he recovers and says, 'No hey buddy come on, don't mess around. That ain't nice. You started to tell me, so ya may as well finish. Come on, what is it you do? Come on for real, huh? Tell me, please?'

I turned to this guy and I said, 'I already told ya, I kill people, that's what I do. For *real*. You want someone *dead*, you call me.' And again I locked eyes with him and he sorta seemed to whither on the spot. Oh boy, he could tell I was being straight then, and the colour just *drained* right out o' his face. I mean, he tried to laugh it off, but I could see he wasn't sure. That's one line o' work I bet he's never had come up before! But he kept hanging on in there, *plugging* away at me, asking question after question. I gave him some facts, so he'd know for sure.

I told him I'd killed *nine* men and three women. It ain't hard to kill someone I said. It ain't the *killin'* that's hard, it's the *getting' away with it*, that's the *hard* part. The other stuff's easy. Ya do your homework and ya find out all you need to find out about the person, and then just work out the best way to do it, and the best time and place to do it. And then just get the job done and walk away. I can kill with a gun, a knife, poison, strangulation ... with my bare hands. I can rig a car to crash; I can create an explosion from every day things you stash in your kitchen. I do what I need to do to get the job done. That's it in a nutshell. It ain't rocket science.

This guy started backing off away from me then and I watched him fumble his cell phone out of his pocket and hurry towards the exit. I mean I could tell just by looking at him he was in a state. *Now* he believed me! *Now* he got the message. But it was a wrong move on my part. I'd had a pretty shit day and I was just playing with him. But I'd let my guard down. I never should have done that. The guy had pissed me off big time and I was just making light of it, I'd just been bragging to see his reaction I guess. So I gave him a few moments to get clear of the place, whilst I used the napkin to wipe my prints from the glass and the counter and then I followed him out. No loose ends. I can't afford no loose ends. *Never. Besides*, ten's an even number. I like that. Neater somehow. Yeah. that's it, neater.

# Cold Dawn

*By Molly Lloyd*

I wake to a cold breeze gently kissing my face. I shiver slightly, suddenly feeling cold all over, that one gentle peck on the cheek spreading to my whole body. *Someone should close that bloody window*, I think to myself. Slowly, I start to open my eyes, but the bright sunlight makes me squeeze them shut again. A dull throbbing pain begins to pool around my eyes, my temples, and the base of my head.

'I'm never drinking again.' I groan, pinching the bridge of my nose to try to relieve my headache.

It doesn't work.

I sigh, putting my hands down, pushing myself into a sitting position. I pause; I'm not on a bed, or even on a sofa. I wrench my eyes open, ignoring the blinding pain bursting throughout my skull. Instead of my familiar bedroom walls I see a stretch of green, only broken up by flashes of white sunbeams.

'Brilliant,' I grumble, 'I'm in a fucking bush.'

Sluggishly, I get onto my hands and knees, and start crawling. Poking my head tentatively out of the leafy curtains, I assess my surroundings. Thankfully, not many people. I exit my bush without losing much more dignity. Now I'm on my feet, I subtly pull down my dress (treacherously bunched around my bum), return my straps to my shoulders and walk the path with purpose. I doubt I'm fooling anyone. But nobody's gawping at me, so clearly I'm not looking too rough. I'm a sight too often seen in this town: a girl who's disgraced herself the night before.

Walking - or rather stumbling - through the park, I try

desperately to remember the night before. It's a blur of colours, shapes and music; each memory I grasp struggles from my grip, like a bubble bursting in my hand. The only thing I'm certain about is the argument with my parents last nightI hope they've forgiven me by the time I get back home.

···

'Dawn! Can you come down here for a moment please?' My father hollered from the bottom of the stairs. I groaned loudly, slamming my make-up box shut. I knew that tone.

'I am a grown woman, for fuck's sake,' I muttered under my breath, stomping down the stairs. Dad was waiting for me, leaning against the bannister. His thick, black eyebrows (now flecked with grey) were furrowed, creating a prominent $V$ in the middle of his forehead. My Dad had always been one of my favourite people: he was always laughing and joking around, and he certainly never frowned. Now I was the one making him look like that. A wave of guilt washed over me. But no, I was not going to be made guilty for having a good time.

'What do you want?' I demanded, stopping on the step above him, but I still had to tilt my head up to look him in the eye. He made me feel so small.

Dad narrowed his clay-brown eyes. Then the flat of his palm smacked the top of the bannister as he turned away from me.

'Come into the living room, please. We need to have a word with you.' Dad led the way; I groaned, jumped off the last step and sauntered into the living room.

My mother was sat in an armchair, her back straight, her delicate hands resting neatly in her lap. She was so tiny in comparison to my father. Again, I felt a temporary wave of guilt . Her petal-like lips were pursed together tightly, and she wouldn't meet my gaze.

'Is this going to take long?' I drawled. 'I'm meant to be getting to Cara's for pre-drinks for 6pm; I want to leave early so I can get some Johnnies on the way.' My statement had the desired effect. Mum's head shot up, her mouth forming a tiny *o*. My father's head whipped round to scowl at me, as he bellowed: 'Dawn!' A smug half smile started to grow on my face as I gave them a tiny shrug.

'Dawn, this has to stop. Your mother and I -' Dad put his massive bear paw of a hand on Mum's shoulder - 'we are really worried about you. We know Matthew hurt you badly -'

'Oh, for fuck's sake -' I mumbled. I did not want to hear that bastard's name. He wasn't in my life anymore, which was absolutely fine by me.

'Please, darling, just listen,' Mum's gentle voice now strained, as if she were in pain, 'If you keep going like this, you're going to get hurt, and we…we… we're just so worried about you, Nugget.' I rolled my eyes after hearing my old pet name. I couldn't bear this any longer. I grabbed my bag and a pair of shoes and hissed: 'Oh would you both get a grip! I am not your little girl who needs saving. Just because I'm not living my life the way *you* want me to, doesn't mean that I'm doing things wrong.' I pointed my bag at them, 'Frankly, I don't think you really give a fuck about me at all! You just want a perfect, obedient daughter to show off to your mates at your golf club and your book club. Well, I'm NOT. I'm going to dance, fuck and drink myself into a stupor, and it's going to be brilliant!'

I turned on my heel and strode towards the door. Just before I walked out, I paused for a moment. Did I want to leave them like this? I didn't really mean anything I'd just said to them. I knew really that they loved me. But every time I shouted at them; I got the same adrenaline rush that I did on a night out. It had become an addiction for me. *Come on, Dawn*, I thought to myself, *make the right choice*. I smiled to myself and called back to them: 'Don't wait up!'

...

Now, he memory of my parents' faces makes me cringe. I can't believe I spoke to them like that. And for what? For me to wake up in a bush after a night out I can't even remember.

'Nice one Dawn. I rub my arms, trying to get some of the warmth back into my limbs. Why didn't I bring a coat?

I'll need to grovel my arse off when I get home. And I need to make some changes in my life. This isn't really how I want to live. I can't keep hurting my parents, my friends and punishing Matthew.

'Oh God, Matthew!' I groan to myself, rubbing my temples. My head is still killing me and no amount temple rubbing can erase the image of Matt's beautiful, kind face looking so angry and hurt.

...

'Dawn don't freak out, but I just saw Matt come into the club,' Cara shouted as we waited for our drinks. Kiera, on my right, looked shocked, her smoky eyes widened, like a Panda Bear. I laughed at them both and shrugged. This didn't fool them for a second. Cara raised a single, dark insinuating eyebrow; Kiera gave me a sideways glance, her concern clear. I hated their pity. I could feel hot anger rising. The anger I had felt with my parents, but I did not want to feel this way. I wanted to feel nothing.

'Here you are girls,' the bartender called, placing down our drinks and 6 shots, 'Take it easy tonight, alright? I'm looking at you, Dawn!' He gave me a little wink. I stuck my tongue out at him.

'No promises!' I shouted, laughing. I knocked back the shots, one after the other, trying to douse the fire inside me.

Looking back, that was a stupid move. Alcohol only fuels a fire.

'Steady on, Dawn!' Kiera laughed, although her eyes still looked concerned.

What a bitch.

'She's right, mate, you've already downed a bottle of Rosé at mine! And you're a lightweight,' Cara chuckled, 'Maybe you should slow down a bit.' There it was again. The worry. Enough was enough.

'Ah, shut up, you grannies,' I said, trying to sound lighter than I felt. I jumped down off my barstool and instantly the room started to rock and spin out of control. 'I'm going to drink as much as I possibly can, and I'm gonna dance with as many 'attractive men as possible! Starting with…' My eyes darted around the club, before resting on a tall man with blonde, slicked back hair. A slight, charming smile was playing on his lips without quite reaching his eyes. They were as dark as thunderclouds, hungry, and they were fixed on me. I could feel heat rise up into my cheeks. I grabbed my drink and flashed him a grin. Pointing, I continued: 'Him!'

I staggered over to the guy, who had already started striding towards me, biting his lip. I threw myself at him, forcing him to catch me in his huge arms. His mouth came down to my ear.

'Boyfriend?' He said, his warm breath tickling my neck. I giggled, pressing my body closer. I looked quickly over his shoulder and, sure enough, I saw Matt glaring at me. *Good*, I thought, smiling wickedly, *this'll prove I've forgotten all about you, you prick*. I brought my hands up behind his neck and tangled my fingers in his hair.

'Nope, I'm all yours,' I slurred back, standing on my tip toes just to reach his ear. He gave me a wolf-like grin and dragged me to the dancefloor.

For hours, all I could see were flashing lights and his dark eyes fixated on me. All I could hear was a cacophony of wailing music, piercing girly screeches and the pounding of feet. I could feel his hands gripping my waist and my arse, crushing me against him. In the end, I was using him like a crutch, as I knew I would crumble to the floor without him.

He mumbled something to me. I stared up at him blankly. His words sounded so jumbled and muffled; I couldn't make them out. He laughed at my confusion, and mouthed the word "drink", waggling an empty glass at me. I nodded obediently, and let him drag me over to a seat, where I practically collapsed, giggling. He smiled down at me, his black eyes looking hungrier than ever, and prowled over to the bar until he was soon engulfed by a swarm of queueing people.

I seemed to just blink, and then suddenly Matt was there, his eyes wide with a mix of anger and concern.

'Dawn, what are you playing at? You're going to kill yourself at this rate! You need to stop,' I tried to push him away but my arms felt like they were filled with wet sand.

'You don't care about me! You left me! *You* left *me*! If you cared, you'd stay and you'd love me and ev'rything,' I slurred. He looked as though I had hit him.

'Dawn, I do care -'

'No, you don't!' I shouted. 'Now, leave! It's what you're good at, isn't it!' Matt clenched his jaw, turned and disappeared into the crowd

Then my new friend was beside me, drinks in hand. 'That didn't look like a fun conversation.' I shook my head and fumbled pathetically with my dress. He smiled 'Here, this'll make you feel better. I guarantee it'll be the best cocktail you'll ever drink.'

. . .

I rub my temples again. That's all I can remember. I grimace as I try and force the memories forward, but no luck.

Not that it matters now. I'm back home. I need to apologise to my parents and Matt and to Cara and Kiera as well. I have been awful to them, and it needs to stop.

As I open the door, I shout to Mum and Dad: 'Hi, I'm home,' I stride forward into the house, 'Sorry I'm back so late, I overdid it last night! You'll never guess where I woke up -' I stop dead in my tracks. They aren't listening to me. They haven't even looked up from the telly.

'Mum, Dad?'

Nothing.

'Look, I know I was a git last night. I'm really sorry, honest! Please don't give me the silent treatment.'

Nothing.

I sigh. The back of my head is still hurting. I reach around and touch where it hurts the most; it feels wet. My hands begin to shake. I slowly bring my hand in front of my face. There's blood.

Is this why I can't remember the rest of last night? Was I attacked? Why didn't I defend myself? Oh god, I took a drink from a stranger, it could have had anything in it. How could I be so stupid?! He could have done anything to me.

'Oh God, oh God, I have to go to the hospital,' I say. My voice shaking almost as much as my hands.Nothing.

'Are you serious? You're ignoring me now? I'm hurt! You are un-fucking-believable! How dare -'

*KNOCK. KNOCK. KNOCK.*

Dad walks past me to the door. I'm too shocked to say anything and watch him, frozen, as he opens the door. There are two police officers in our doorway.

'Good morning, sir, are you the father of Dawn Wight?' One asks stiffly.

'Officer, I'm Dawn Wight! I think I was atta -' I start to say, before I'm interrupted.

'Yes, I am, although Dawn isn't home right now. Is she alright?'

'Dad I'm right here! What's happening?' Hysteria bubbles up inside, trying to rip its way out.

The other officer coughs, shifting his weight from one foot to the other. 'May we come in, sir? It's best if your wife hears this as well.' Dad leads them into the living room, and I follow. Mum looks up, a million questions in her eyes.

'I'm sorry to tell you this, Mr and Mrs Wight, but we found your daughter's body this morning. It appears she was attacked last night, and suffered a blow to the head, which she did not survive. We're so very sorry for your loss.'

Fuck.

# Run, Rabbits, Run

*By Judy Birkbeck*

The sun streamed in. Mike had already left for work. I
put on Nick Cave's Murder Ballads. No need to leave for
two hours. Vacillating, I was vacillating. I could live here.
Me and Mike, together. A role, an identity ready-made.
The garden was manicured, a berry-dropping young elder
tree the only hint of untidiness, and beyond were fields of
immaculate green grass or golden corn. All so clean, no
litter here. The silence was so profound I could hear the
workings of my inner ears. A strange magic hush, pleasant
after the siren strains of Hackney. Was this what I needed
after all? A mackerel sky promised change. Mackerel sky,
mackerel sky, never long wet, never long dry.

On the desk was a present wrapped in silver foil bearing
my name. Inside was his grandmother's ring and a note: I
love you, Nicole. I think of you all the time. Text me when
you arrive home safely. Love you lots. Mike. Bless. And
bless again. A surge of love went through me.

While texting back my eye wandered to a folder marked
Life Essences. Curiosity about Mike's job overcame me.
An hour later I was trembling, and the blood drummed in
my ears like the thumping from a warren underfoot, loud,
and angry and shouting to be heard more than anything
else. I read that in a study of analgesics rats were placed
in holders with their tails taped to the laboratory table
and electrically stimulated via two hypodermic needles
which remained in place for six hours, with an increase in
voltage till a vocalisation was elicited. Till they screamed,
the author meant. I read: following anaesthesia with
pentobarbital sodium … heparin was injected into the

inferior vena cava: the heart was rapidly excised, and the aorta cannulated. Arcane descriptions that hid the reality of the dying creatures, minimised their significance, euphemised the atrocity and coated it with a gloss of sound science. Animals as data. I read that tissues were *harvested* from *donors*. Harvested: the word evoked images of rural bounty, golden cornfields in the view through the window, apples piled high in the market. Donors: willing givers of something precious, selfless benefactors of their fellows. I read a letter from a breeding firm boasting of the gentle nature of its dogs and hence suitability for experimentation. I read that rabbits with ulcerated sores were not treated but killed and *bled out*. I read of a year-long insecticide experiment which described *very thin, ill-looking dogs, very timid, many extremely scared.* I read a record sheet showing that two-thirds of rats and mice bred were gassed as surplus stock – others were disposed of as *non-conforming products* or *no longer of prime breeding age* or because they had devoured their young, thus sparing them the trauma of their parents. I read that vast numbers of rabbits were used to test for skin irritation by detergents, in the eyes, and I thought of the hoarding back home that boasted of a new-formula detergent for Better-Brighter-Cleaner-Whiter clothes. Washes out blood stains. I read accounts of procedures with no mention of any human agent – things were done to the animals as if by magic, and the hand of the perpetrator was in every case unseen. I read of lesions and perfusions and irradiations and excisions of parts as if they had not belonged to living creatures. I read of the frequent and mysterious *inability to assay*. I read that animals were *sacrificed, lost through intraoperative exsanguination, investigated under terminal anaesthesia, anaesthetised, and then exsanguinated*, subjected to *Craniocervical dislocation*. No. They didn't do those things. Let's be clear. They killed them.

On the shelf stood a video marked Life Essences. I slotted it into the machine. A dog lay anaesthetised on its back on a paper towel-covered table while two white-coated men fastened leg and body straps. The dog shifted its head. The two donned rubber gloves and assembled instruments on a tray. The camera shifted upwards, and Mike's face came into view on the left. In the silence broken only by the clink of instruments and rustle of clothes I had not realised the volume was on loud till the scalpel cut into the dog's abdomen and an ear-splitting squeal filled the room. The dog kicked violently.

Mike laughed.

'This dog could have been out a bit more.'

'Nah', said his colleague, 'this won't take long.'

Mike inserted a scissor clamp under a piece of gut to keep it exposed and the pair set to work. Two puddles of dark red blood collected in its outstretched ears. The eyeballs rolled and turned pink. With tongs they took out organ after organ while I sat mesmerised and deafened for an eternity and the dog kicked and squealed, kicked, and squealed, kicked, and squealed. At the end, the dog lay still. The two men ripped off gloves and left.

I cried and cried, for the animals and for myself and my dead gran and the screaming pigs and silent lambs in the animal wagons on the way here, as if all the grief I had ever known was coming back like heartburn, hurting all over again.

I left a note next to the ring: Thanks anyway, but I can't take it.

I exploded onto the road home.

*

There was no plaque on the hillside building, but one of Ceri's friends scented the whiff of ammonia after we cut through the chain-link fence topped with barbed wire. Two people stayed as lookouts in case of a silent alarm. There were no windows, but the door yielded to club hammer and cold chisel.

We stood frozen. Racks of white rabbits in stocks, four tiers high, six to a tier, filled the room. Ninety-six rabbits stared with barely an ear twitch. They were silent. By the dim torchlight I saw the eyes bleeding or swollen and ulcerated. Their eyes made no protest for the ultimate in laundry care or lawn perfection. We wept. Who would give them a voice, them and those which would surely take their place next week and every week?

Ceri and I undid the neck locks while the others went into the next room. One by one we unclamped them and placed them on the floor where they stayed, unaccustomed to moving, till at last, when the floor was full, they began to shift and scurry. Just as I had the last one in my hands, the torch battery ran out, Ceri whipped out a lighter and flicked, the rabbit kicked, I fell against the front door, the door opened, and the kerfuffle resulted in a panicking mob. I smiled as a stream of rabbits poured through the doorway and hopped over my supine form. We had argued fiercely whether to release them and risk spreading unknown infection to wildlife populations – my preference, for which I was rightly called irresponsible – or to take them away to be further incarcerated, even if less unkindly. I had accidentally won the argument.

The others were coming out, loaded with boxes which they carried to the cars. Ceri replaced the torch battery and we walked through a bead curtain to the back rooms – no, not a bead curtain, it was made of rats' tails strung together. In an ominously labelled handling room were shelves stacked with black bin liners and yellow plastic sacks, and a ceiling-high refrigerator bearing a sign: All animals placed in this refrigerator must be dead. No similar notice was on the furnace. On the wall was a Playboy centrefold. In other rooms were wall-to-wall cages of rabbits with raging raw wounds in their sides. They stared. We took them out in boxes. Likewise, the rats and mice with babies, or pregnant. Five beagle puppies cowered in individual cages, pressed against the furthest bars. Bodies and bare concrete floors were smeared with faeces. All was silent. The puppies were wiped, wrapped, and stuffed down five jacket fronts. Alone in one of the offices, I found myself drawn to a photo on the desk. Me and Mike with his arm round me. Me smiling.

The theatre was bare: the wooden table with the metal tray on top, leg and body straps dangling, instruments exposed on a shelf, spotlights hanging from the ceiling, a drip rack. Bare, but in my mind, I saw a dog kicking and squealing. I heard Mike laughing and saying, this dog could have been out a bit more, and the colleague saying, No, this won't take long. I wrenched myself away and fetched the club hammer from outside. One by one the rabbits were finding their way through the hole in the chain-link fence. I went back in. I saw rabbits with swollen eyelids and raw bleeding sides and muck-covered puppies and a dog kicking and squealing and I smashed the stocks, I brought the hammer down with both hands. One by one I smashed them all. I went through and saw a dog kicking and squealing and I smashed the computers, I smashed the photo of me and Mike, I smashed the rabbit cages, I smashed the bars of the puppy cages. I went into the theatre and saw a dog kicking and squealing, kicking and squealing, kicking and squealing, kicking and squealing, kicking and squealing... Ceri grabbed my raised arm and shone her torch on the shattered remains of light bulbs and fittings, leg strap fixtures, scalpels and tongs and drip rack scattered over the floor.

'Don't forget the rats and mice,' she said.

'What rats and mice?'

She led me back to the room with the rabbit stocks, where the others were pulling out drawers from floor-to-ceiling racks. The stench of ammonia hit me then. Some lay dead, their water bottles drained into the sawdust – the floor of one drawer was so wet, the sawdust was floating. Some had bitten lumps out of each other. Some staggered with advanced sickness. Food hoppers contained smelly blue mould, and two of them heaved with maggots. We put the sick and injured in boxes and released the rest. No room in the cars. In such a small building we had not expected so many. They soon ran. We shooed the last few rabbits, standing with learned helplessness, towards the fence hole. I stepped outside the fence, stood in the moonlight, and watched them go.

Run, rabbits, run. You matter too. Stretch your legs, shake out your ears, have brief but happy lives. Taste the grass moistened with dew, feel the vapour-laden air swish in your eyes instead of the latest, brightest-washing detergent. Turn your heads whichever way you want. Run and kick, kick hard, kick as you have never kicked before, not once in your lives, feel the power in your back legs, feel the ground recede under your feet. See the moon and its fluid tree shadows shorten and lengthen. And if you live, see the fullness of the day, the disc that illuminates the sky, let the radiance fill your heads, shine on your sore eyes, heal your weeping wounds. Look across the skies and see the clouds drift, see horizons, and go there, then see more horizons. They belong to you. This is your world too. Out there is more, so much more. Smell the smells and hear the thumping of your born-free cousins underground. That could be you. Feel the hardness as you sink your teeth into wood, feel rain and then feel the warm sun again. You will not have far to go. But when the sparrowhawks or the owls take you, you will at least have had a life. Go, run for all your predecessors and their short, tortured lives, all your successors and the hopes and promises that hang unfulfilled over their heads. Run for the offspring you will never have. Run, rabbits, run.

I stood on the hillside and watched as the last of the timid white creatures hop-stopped away from the fence then, gathering confidence and speed, ran to the shelter of the nearby woodland or guilelessly across the open fields. In the moonlight a hundred gleaming white blips radiated out across the landscape like dropped ball bearings speeding down the faces of the hill. I felt a tug at my sleeve.

'Come on', said Ceri. 'It's finished.'

'We'll be your voice,' I murmured.

# The Red Shoes

*By John Ward*

She came into my office, no advance call. Just knocked on
the door and walked in. We'll call her April, between you
and me. No real names here, you understand. April breezed
in and sat down, but only after I'd moved a pile of papers
to the floor.

'Sorry,' I said, 'no space.' I don't usually apologise to
anyone, but April was the sort of person you felt inferior to
straight away.

She had walked up four flights to my office. The
elevator was stuck again. Yet, she was still looking cool.
Long legs in heeled shoes, tight skirt, waisted grey jacket
and a small black hat with one feather. Her perfume wafted
in behind her, but delicately. Forty years old, I guessed.
She clearly took care of her appearance. I would call her a
sophisticated lady compared with my usual clients.

'How can I help you?' I said.

Sometimes a lady would talk and her problems would
come racing towards me in a rush of words. Not April.

'You won't be helping me. You'll be doing as I tell you,'
she said. The tone of our working relationship had been set.

I know what you're thinking. You're thinking this is
going to be April's story. It isn't, but you should know what
she was like, it has a bearing.

My line of work is full of surprises. All these years,
spying on other people's lives, learning secrets I'd rather
not know, hiding on street corners for days on end or
driving hundreds of miles for no reward.

I've seen it all. If you know what I know of human
nature, you may wonder at the futility of life too.

Don't get me wrong. I don't have all the answers. I can only tell you how it is.

Yet, now and again, something will happen that will knock me sideways, will make me question whether I have seen it all. After all, I could be wrong. You'll have to make up your own mind. I'll tell you the story and you can give me your opinion. It won't make any difference to me, but I'd like to hear it anyway.

The case outlined by April sounded standard stuff. Wife suspects husband, wants him followed, wants a report on a weekly basis, she'll take it from there. In fact, she'll probably take him for all he's got. Not too interesting a case for me but, hey, I have to pay the rent.

April tells me, 'George, my husband, is not to be trusted.'

'You don't trust him in what way?'

'That's for you to find out,' she said. 'That's what I'm paying you for.' There's no arguing with April. You learn not to be judgemental in this job. Reality is rarely as it appears on the surface.

I took the job. Three-quarter payment, cash up front and full employment for a month. George was easy enough to track. He managed his own construction company, filed for his taxes on time every year, was making good money, bank account in credit, investments in place. Treated his workers well, no outstanding debt. Don't ask me how I know this. I have ways of finding out.

Personally, below April's class. I can see why she might want to detach herself from George. Overweight, doesn't dress well, nearing fifty but looking older, losing his hair. Maybe she found him unlike her usual friends, more rough and ready, but now she's bored with him. He works too hard, doesn't pay her enough attention. She wants more out of life. I can guess at motives but in this business only facts count.

Fact is I couldn't find anything about George that would lead April to think he couldn't be trusted.

Sure, he didn't come home too soon after his day finished; went to a bar some days, usually alone, never with a woman. Didn't seem in a hurry to get home to April but, hey, that's how some marriages work.

I followed George for three weeks. Sat in my car, stood on street corners, sat discreetly in the same bars. Nothing happened. I reported to April when she phoned me.

She'd say, 'Anything?'

I'd say, 'Nothing.' That was the extent of our conversations.

Now, in case you're thinking that this is George's story, you'll be glad to know it isn't.

The month was nearly up. I was due to report back to April. She would pay for the remainder for my time, she'd accept she had nothing on George, we'd part company and I'd look for my next job. That's what I thought.

I had one more day to trail George. Remember I told you that now and again something happens to knock you sideways. This was that day. This is my story now.

I trailed George from his office to a late night diner in Downtown. It was already dark. He'd not come here before. Businesses are shuttered for the night. Nobody is on the streets because the rain is sheeting down, and it's Wednesday night.

George parks by the roadside a block away. I've found a space at the last corner, hoping he doesn't get out but goes home instead.

I say, aloud, in the safe cocoon of my car, 'Go home, George. I've had enough. Go home to April,' hoping that the power of thought will transmit my message to him. It doesn't. He gets out, puts his hat on, pushes his collar up and walks to the diner. I follow, like a shadow image. He pushes the door open and walks in.

I can't follow him. It would be too obvious. The diner reminds me of that famous Edward Hopper painting, Nighthawks, You must know it; everybody does. Big picture window, blue interior. It's where lonely souls go at night.

George takes his hat and coat off, gives them a shake, puts them on a stool and plants himself on the next one. The man behind the counter comes to talk to George. My thought waves say, 'Sorry, Sir, I'm just closing, come back tomorrow.' Again, it doesn't work. I make a mental note to work on thought transmission, starting tomorrow.

George is served a large mug of something and a pastry.

I huddle into my coat, pull my hat down, lean against the wall and prepare for a cold, wet time.

I'm thinking, 'George, why don't you go home? What's keeping you out?' I realise that, after a month of surveillance, I don't know George at all. I don't know what he thinks about or why he doesn't go home, but that isn't my brief. I'm only being paid to follow him and report his actions, not his thoughts.

My thoughts are interrupted. I've been here twenty minutes, sheltering against the rain. Nobody has come by, but now there is a woman, standing on the opposite corner. I didn't see her arrive, I was busy watching George. She takes my attention. She'd take anyone's attention. Is she here for George? Maybe she is the reason I'm standing here in the rain.

It was the red shoes that attracted me. All around her was grey, wet, cold but the red shoes shone out like a beacon.

They were attached by slim, shapely legs to a body. It would have been good to see her body, because the legs were sensational and there was every reason to suppose that the body would be sensational too.

It was enclosed in a black leather-look raincoat, the type that should be leather but you know it isn't because it's too shiny. Shiny with the material but also with the rain that was teeming down. The coat was gathered at the waist with a belt, tied not buckled, but you just knew the waist it was tied around was young, slim, like the legs.

I couldn't see her face because she held a small umbrella. Enough to hide her face, but not enough to keep the rain off her coat and red shoes.

Her hair was dark, long, under a rain hat, leather-look, like the raincoat.

The lights from the diner shimmered in the rain and, occasionally, a car would whoosh past, throwing light and shadows on this girl waiting in the rain.

I was fascinated by her. How long would she wait? Who was she waiting for? Maybe for me. Should I walk across and ask her?

A man walks past. She pays him no mind, but I see that he turns and looks at this girl in the red shoes. He can't know why she is standing in the rain, waiting, because he turns again and moves on. She's not waiting for him, but is she waiting for me?

I have to tear my attention away from her and I glance over to George. He's gone! Where's he gone? Did he come out the door? Did I miss him? I don't think so. Maybe he's gone to the men's room. No, his hat and coat have gone too. My eyes scan the diner. No sign of George. Damn, I've lost him. I was obsessing over the girl.

I look back to her. She's gone too. Where did she go? I've lost both of them. What shall I do? Go home? Look for the girl?

No, I'll be the professional I think I am. I'll find where

George went.

I cross the street and enter the diner. There's no one in there except the owner, preparing to close down. He says, 'Sorry, Sir, we're just closing. Come back tomorrow.' My thought waves, meant for George, have taken twenty minutes to cross the street.

'No, I don't want anything but can you tell me where that man went?'

'What man, buddy?'

'The one sitting at the counter for the past twenty minutes.'

'I don't remember nobody, buddy.'

'I was waiting for him. He left a few minutes ago but I didn't see him go.'

'No, doesn't ring a bell with me.'

I give him twenty dollars.

'Oh, him. Why didn't you say? Told me someone was outside waiting for him and was there another way out? He went through my kitchen and out the back door. Is he hiding from you?'

'Where?'

'Back there.'

I run through to where he's pointing and push the back door open.

There's something heavy behind it and the door doesn't open fully. I push harder and the weight moves. I ease my way through. It's George. I stare at him before bending to feel for a pulse. Nothing. I look at my hand and can see, even in this murky light, that it's covered in blood.

'You bastard, George, why didn't you go home?'

Before I stand up the cops arrive.

The diner owner has called them. After the paramedics attend to George, the police sit us down, the diner man and me, and go through our stories. My story, even to me, doesn't sound too good.

The owner tells them George was fleeing from someone waiting outside.

I tell them the truth, even about the girl. 'Who was she and where is she now?' they want to know. I don't have an answer.

They ask the diner man about her, but he never saw a girl. The only person waiting outside was me, except in my version of events.

The cops arrest me on suspicion, handcuff me and take me away.

It's now a month later. I'm still in custody, charged with murder. Several people have testified that they saw me trailing George, in various places. Others testify that I've been asking questions about George. April denies any knowledge of me. She has a watertight alibi for that night.

It looks bad for me. No one else is implicated. All the cops lack is a motive. The girl in the red shoes has not been found. They say I dreamed her up. Maybe I did. I still obsess about her. Sometimes events can knock you sideways, can make you change the way you view the world.

Could I have stopped these events? Could I have handled it differently? I don't know, but I may have plenty of time to reflect.

You've heard my story. What do you think? You'll have to make up your own mind.

# The Satchel Bag

*By Stephen Wade*

Like an opportunistic killer hiding in the shadows, Damian Thompson stood on the bottom step next to one of the iconic shopfront's pilasters. Despite the early winter sunset, he wore dark-lensed glasses. The lenses corrected so he could see clearly the woman he had targeted on the online dating site. Through the shouts of the city traders threatening the last of the aftershave and celebrity T-shirts, Thompson homed in on the ping in his satchel messenger bag.

He pulled out his phone, and, without opening the message, read the words, 'Sorry Damian, I won't be able …' His phone pinged again. And again. And another two times. He hated the way people divided every sentence into single messages.

Okay, time enough had elapsed. Now he could read the full message without seeming too eager.

'Sorry Damian, I won't be able to make it on time,' the full first line of the first message read. He opened the second: 'I'm still on the train.' The third: 'There was a technical delay.' And the last two: 'I'll be there soon.' The last message was two kissing emojis with red love hearts.

Thompson smiled.

He had her. With the advantage of him being on time and this woman running late, this one would be easy. The woman's guilt would put him in a position of superiority.

For a while Thompson watched the conveyor belt of pedestrians until the daylight faded too much for him to continue wearing his sunglasses. Not that he cared about what others thought, but it was too dark to make anything out clearly. With no case to put them in, Thompson hung the sunglasses on his T-shirt collar by one of the glasses' arms. Putting them in his satchel bag risked damaging them.

Unable now to see anyone, he pulled out his phone, opened up the dating site and checked out the two or three latest females who had shown interest in him. One in her forties had sent him a message. He ignored it. Another two had liked his profile - one from France the other from Asia. He opened up the Profile of the Asian woman, but ignored the one from France.

'Hi,' a female voice said to his left and slightly behind him.

Thompson looked up, the practised smile on his face. 'Hey,' he said. 'You must be Jennifer.'

The woman smiled too, but it wavered a bit. She held out her hand. 'Hi,' she repeated. 'Sorry I'm late. But, like I said ...'

Thompson took her hand, told her there was no problem, and eased her towards him. She yielded, so he kissed her on both cheeks. Something he'd picked up from a few years living abroad. The woman pressed her cheeks into his kisses. Her eyes smiled.

'You look nice,' he said, deliberately letting his eyes slide down her body to her feet and clambering back to her chest. He knew what worked.

'So do you,' she said.

Thompson swallowed. 'Are you hungry?'

The woman smiled an upside down smile. And she bobbed her head a few times. 'Maybe,' she said, and gave a short laugh, 'just a cake and a coffee.'

Perfect. Everything was going as Thompson had planned. The bookshop café was one of his favourite haunts. He told her there was a café inside, if she was okay with that. She was. He held the door open for her.

On the moving stairs in front of them, a guy in his twenties. With his hands resting on the moving banisters, he looked to Thompson like a prick that needed to be taught a lesson. If he were on his own, Thompson would have pushed past him with a curt 'watch out there'.

'Are you okay?' the female called Jennifer said.

Why wouldn't he be okay? People were always trying to undermine others, always trying to assess them. 'Yeah,' he said. 'I'm fine.'

In the café, she said she'd have an Americano.

'Sure,' he said. He then ordered. 'An Americano and a decaf Americano, please.' And then back to the woman with him. 'What cake would you like?'

'I'll have this one,' she said, pointing to an almond slice. 'If you'll eat half of it.'

Some of the coffee spilled from the coffees into the saucers as he was carrying the tray to a table. How the hell did waiters manage to avoid spilling drinks?

When they sat down, he used napkins to sop up the spilled coffee. The offensive, brown napkins he left on the tray, which he placed on another table.

'So,' Thompson said, 'This is where we ask each other about what we like to do in our free time and stuff.' He deliberately left a pause to see how she'd handle it. She smiled a disarming smile in response and tilted her head.

'I'm just kidding,' he said. 'But, how about this? If you were being interviewed on the TV or on radio, what types of questions would you like to be asked?'

Her mouth shifted into a turned-down smile. She threw the question back at him. 'You tell me,' she said. 'What questions would you like?'

'I don't know,' he said. 'I guess it'd depend on who was doing the interviewing.'

'Who would you like to be interviewed by?' she said.

Thompson allowed himself one of the many smiles he'd practised in front of his bathroom mirror. A smile he considered enigmatic.

'You,' he said.

She laughed, her head tilted back engagingly. 'Okay,' she said. 'What are you looking for in a potential girlfriend?'

About to say 'You' again – too pedestrian - he checked himself. Instead he described the woman he was talking with. Her height, age and shape, and the type of clothes she was wearing.

This made the permanent smile on her face even wider. A strange pain caught him in the chest. He used the side of his thumb to wipe away sweat from his upper lip. This wasn't how he was supposed to feel. He tried to find something about her that annoyed him: The way she ate, the slurping sounds as she tipped back her coffee cup, the way the white cuff on her shirt rested on the wet coffee saucer. But none of this bothered him.

'I need to go to the ladies,' she said. She opened her handbag and checked something inside, closed her bag and stood up. 'Don't run off on me now.' That incredible smile again.

Thompson watched her move off the way a stalking tiger might regard an antelope too distant to prey-rush. If he had had a tail, he would have swished it. That's when he noticed she'd left her blue jacket sitting on the back of her chair. Without knowing what he might be looking for, he placed his hands inside one of its pockets - nothing. Then the other: a tissue and a receipt.

But wait, there was something in the inside pocket. He could feel the weight of it as he shifted the coat on the back of the chair. Putting his hands behind his neck, he twisted his head in a way that he could shift his eyes about the café. Nobody was looking his way. The something in the woman's inside pocket was a notebook. Thompson slipped it out and opened it. The most recently used pages had quite a few names of men that appeared to have been taken from online dating sites. There were comments next to their details. What her impression of them was. How meetings went. And some of them had ticks and smiley faces, while others exes and sad or angry emojis. His was the last profile name and details in the notebook. Next to his photo was a question mark.

In his peripheral vision, he could see the white of her top returning. He slipped the notebook back into the pocket.

'Hi Jason,' she said. 'I'm back.'

'Hey,' he said. This was the first time she'd used the name 'Jason', the one he'd chosen for the online dating site. He never put up the same details twice on any profile. He told her he felt like going somewhere else. He had in mind the quiet little park behind the concert hall. Even in the summertime, there were always secluded parts where a guy could bring a girl without anybody bothering him. Where the muffled cries of a struggling woman with a hand placed over her mouth could go undetected - except by the birds and the squirrels.

She agreed without hesitation. As a blow-in, she said she'd leave it up to him. Thompson suggested they just go take some fresh air. Walk about for a bit. Then maybe go get something to eat somewhere.

'You're the boss,' she said, and saluted.

Thompson found himself smiling with her, a smile that he didn't have to fake. Taking hold of his satchel bag, he said he had to use the toilet himself first. Instinctively, he picked up his satchel.

'You don't trust me?' she said, indicating the bag in his hands.

Thompson's immediate reaction was to protest and make up something about having tablets or medicine in the bag. But quick thinking told him this might in some way undermine him as a lesser human being - a sickly one.

'Just a habit,' he said. He placed it back down on the chair he'd been sitting in.

Even as he worked his way around the tables to the toilets, Thompson clenched his teeth till they hurt. What if this female opened his bag? Why hadn't he just smiled at her, made no excuse and took the bloody bag with him? The urge to twist about and see if she was in fact going through the bag attacked him like an itch. But using all his willpower, he remained focused on getting to the toilets. Besides, were he to turn around, his weak eyesight would let him down.

When he returned to the mezzanine café, Thompson squinted in an attempt to locate the table with the woman. But all the tables were occupied. He couldn't be sure which one he'd been sitting at. About to do a turnabout, make his way to the exit and phone her, he spotted his jacket on the back of the chair where he thought he'd been sitting. The two middle-aged men quit their yapping and eyed him through their dopey glasses as he approached.

'Is that my jacket?' Thompson said to one of them, or both of them, or neither.

The men looked at him the way onlookers might regard a too-loud drunk in the streets at night. Inside Thompson, a heated sensation flared up. The feeling that always came before he did something that was outside his own control. But luckily, for him, and for the two men, one of them lifted his jacket off the back of the chair and handed it to him.

'Thanks,' he said, clenched his lips and nodded. About to ask them if they'd seen a woman leave from the table, he twisted about and made his way to the exit.

Before leaving the shop, he put on his corrected-lenses-sunglasses and moved about between the different aisles of books on the ground floor. Within minutes, some dopey security guard, as lanky as he was skinny, was following him. This, Thompson put down to his wearing the sunglasses, and to what he could feel was his own shiftiness.

Out in the street, Thompson spotted two cops walking towards him, a male and a female. What an idiot he'd been. Why hadn't he just got himself out of the shop as soon as he'd realised this one had got away? Readying himself for a sprint, he unzipped his jacket, slipped off his glasses and put them in his inside pocket. But as the cops neared him, he could see that they were smiling and more interested in their own conversation than responding to any formal report his would-be date had made. But Thompson knew how the police operated. Personal experience of previous accusations and arrests, along with what he had learned over the years from having a father in the force gave him special insight.

At home that evening, Thompson sat before the TV watching but not really taking in much of what was happening on CBS Reality's Medical Detectives. His mind was more preoccupied with whether or not the woman who had stolen his bag would report him to the police when she went through its contents: among them a scissors, duct tape, and specially enhanced knee pads to withstand kneeling on rough ground.

Printed in Great Britain
by Amazon